To Tamar
From Tina

My BALD IS Beautiful

I Am Not My Hair

May you be enspired by these
Stories to own your bald
journey.

Best Regards,

My Bald Is Beautiful: I Am Not My Hair

One Kingdom Publishing books may be ordered through booksellers or by contacting:

Michele Irby Johnson
www.iam-mij.com
www.onekingdompublishing.com
(301) 453-4770

Because of the dynamic nature of the internet, any web address or links contained in this book may have changed since publication and may no longer be valid. The views expressed in this work are solely those of the author and do not necessarily reflect the views of the publisher, and the publisher hereby disclaims any responsibility for them.

Any people depicted in stock imagery provided by SPJ Graphics are models, and such images are being used for illustrative purposes only.

Cover Design by SPJ Graphic Designs || spjgraphicdesigns.com || (301) 720-2039

ISBN: 979-8-9850350-1-8

Printed in the United States of America

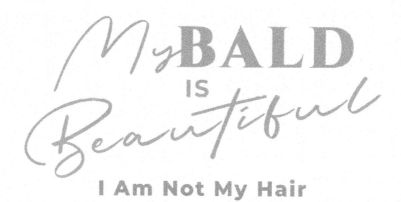

I Am Not My Hair

Table of Contents

Co-Author Dedications

☙ • ❧

SummahLuv Alston

I dedicate this book to my mother, Sarah Frances Patricia Ann Lingard Alston! Even though she was strong enough to have so many names, she lost her battle to breast cancer at the young age of 51! Mom... If only I would have known that she was an alopecia patient as a result of the chemotherapy treatments as a cancer patient, I would have purposely shaved my head in support of her before she passed! Missing her every day, I continue to grow through her love, words, and fond memories! And for that I thank and love you eternally! This one's for you, Mommy!

☙ • ❧

Lisa D. Barnes

To the handsome guy in Walmart, whose genuine compliment (just two weeks after going bald) on my hair cut, head shape and of course my big brown eyes solidified my commitment on becoming Bald, Bold, and Beautiful!!!

◯**•**◯

Sheila Belle

I dedicate this book to my mother, Rose Belle, who is the strongest woman I know. She has modeled love, sacrifice, faithfulness, and determination in her daily walk. Her faith walk has inspired me to press pass the pain and keep God first in all that I do. Because of her I live. I love you, Mommy!

◯**•**◯

Yummekia Boggon

I dedicate this book to my wonderful husband, William Boggon and to my awesome children, Bridney Williams, Brandus Williams, Elijah Williams and Imani Boggon, Allison Boggon, Breanna Boggon and William Boggon, Jr. I am who I am today because of you all! Your love and support keep me grounded. When I want to throw in the towel, your love says NO! You guys push me. You all helped me to believe in myself and because of that my dreams are coming to fruition! My love for you all is FOREVER!!!

◯**•**◯

Carol Chisolm

I dedicate this book to those beautiful bald women in my life who inspired me to embrace my bald journey. Whether it was your graceful glide across the gym or your witty words of wisdom, you encouraged me to live my reality out loud and unapologetically. I'm forever grateful to you Tonia, Gina, and Ariel.

$\infty \bullet \infty$

Juanita Contee
I dedicate this book to my five beloved children, Jade, Jizelle, Jude, Jacob, and Jamison, Jr. Being your mother makes life worth living. Thank you for loving mommy unconditionally, even in the toughest of times. Mommy loves you all forever and always.

$\infty \bullet \infty$

LaQuisha Jackson
I dedicate this book to my BIG brother, LaVar Edward Bagley, Sr., who always told me that I was "crazy" if I didn't think I was BEAUTIFUL. Because of you, I know now, more than ever what it means to really LOVE MYSELF and to truly live on PURPOSE! Thank you for being you. I love and miss you always. Continue to watch over us. Forever YOUR ~Lil Ugly.

$\infty \bullet \infty$

Arlene McGuire
This work is dedicated to my grandmother, Muriel Gray, who left us in 1992 at the age of 95. My desire to be a woman of God has been instilled in me from her example. I try daily to toe the line she lived before me. This work is also dedicated to my mother, Thelma Markland, who left us in 2012 at the age of 82. She is still my inspiration for all that she achieved over her entire life. I was removed from my mother's life early on after my birth. She contracted Polio Myelitis and her left arm was crippled because in

iii

1930 there was no cure for this disease. My grandmother became my mother. Their teachings and examples are an integral part of my wisdom today. I know that their prayers brought me through many storms of early life. Even now, I believe from their transcendence they are still keeping me lifted up.

 C3 • 80

Annie Mewborne

First and foremost, I dedicate this book to God, Whose gifts allow me to empower and inspire the lives of others. Second, to my Aunt Ida Jean Mabry, who always through her prayers and words of encouragement, continues to believe in me when I sometimes fail to believe in myself. To my children: Yakim, (La)Mesha, and Immanuel – your Momma continues to achieve the impossible. You three are my heart, heartbeat, and air. Thank you for your unending love and understanding. To my muse – the fierce Sista Kimberly Carey, who spoke harsh truths, gentle words, telling me to get out of my way, OWN IT and embrace my fierceness! Lastly, to my bald sisters everywhere who continue to suffer in silence – I challenge you all to Be Bald...Be Bold...Be Bodacious!

C3 • 80

Theresa "Tee" Sudderth

I dedicate this book to the ever-broadening movement committed to the awareness, understanding and acceptance of alopecia and its many forms. For the sister struggling with this disease, hold on, have faith and patience. I promise you – you will come out on the other side victorious.

 C3 • 80

Stephanie White

I dedicate this book to all the beautiful sisters who are struggling in their own skin. Whether it's with your hair or with weight, know that you are beautiful just the way you are. You are not your hair. Your hair is an extension of your beauty. Stand tall and be BOLD!

C3 • 80

Shurvone Wright

I dedicate this book to my husband, Roger Wright, my daughter's Danielle, Destiny and Rebekah Wright; and my grand-daughter, Naielle Natnael, who without them I would not have made it. Your love and support give me motivation to keep going when things in life get hard. I am encouraged to take bold and courageous moves in life to show you that anything is possible, and that you can be all that God has created you to be. I also want to dedicate this book to all the women who might be afraid to be unique, bald, and bold. I encourage you to stand in your beauty, and strength and know that you are amazing and powerful.

C3 • 80

Michele Zaret

I dedicate this story to my family who has always been a very loving and caring support system for me.

My Bald Is Beautiful: I Am Not My Hair

Foreword

Cʒ•ꙄꙄ

As women, we live our lives on a rollercoaster. Seemingly, we are built for the myriad of ups and down, and unplanned turnarounds. We face changes of varying degrees on a daily basis and for the most part we can navigate what comes our way with strength, tenacity, and resilience. We have an innate ability to bounce back from whatever life throws our way. We can balance children, careers, spouses, school, entrepreneurship, community service, health challenges, and spiritual relationships with God, all the while keeping it all together…Not a hair out of place! But what happens when our hair – our glory, the element that gives us that personality, that sassiness, that uniqueness, that flare – fights against us and ultimately fails us?

Can you imagine the unexpected turn that life takes when a woman loses her hair? That is not to say that hair loss it not a tragic reality for men. Women can just about handle any form of loss, but to discover that our hair is falling out and it is not expected to ever grow back is devastating to say the least. Hair loss to any degree brings about a multitude of emotions from low self-esteem, shame, anger, fear, and depression. While some women choose to shave their hair off, many others are blindsided with medical conditions that strip them of their hair – conditions such as cancer, medically induced hair loss, or alopecia. Alopecia is an autoimmune disease in which your immune system attacks your hair follicle and hair loss occurs usually involving the scalp, and at times every hair on your body. This disease affects 6.8 million people in the U.S. 147 million people world-wide.

I invite you to take a journey and read these amazing stories of women that are Bald, Bold, and Beautiful. As they share their real-life experiences through hair loss, it is the hope of this literary work that you will walk away with a greater understanding and acceptance that you are *not* your hair!

Jamie Elmore
Editor in Chief Bald Life Magazine

JAMIE ELMORE

Jamie Elmore is a hairstylist, salon owner of J Salon in Seattle, Washington and has worked in the industry for 30 years. Despite her professional experience, she struggled with hair loss.

In 1998, Jamie found her first bald spot. Prior to Jamie's alopecia diagnosis from her doctor in 2004, she had never seen or heard of this disease. Jamie suffered in silence for years. Her doctor prescribed an array of medications for depression and self-induced panic attacks. She was living a "Masquerade." As a hairstylist she could not fix herself.

In 2006, she gained the courage to shave the remaining hair from her head. After a life-changing meeting with an eleven-year-old little girl suffering from the same condition, Jamie was compelled to start the Alopecia Support Group in 2009, so that others would know they are not alone.

The Alopecia Support Group is a Nonprofit organization that provides – but is not limited to – retreats, one-on-one and group coaching, writing, team building, exercise, workshops, and global pen pals.

In 2020, Jamie published Bald Life Magazine which features men, women, and children from every corner of the world that are living with hair loss due to alopecia, cancer, medically induced or simply by choice. The magazine is a platform for bald individuals to heal, find their voice, and share their stories.

Jamie is the founder of the Alopecia Support Group, Founder of the Bald Boss, a motivational speaker, writer, alopecia confidence coach, radio producer, executive producer of a documentary entitled "Harmony" alopecia stories, Editor in Chief of Bald Life Magazine, Soul Café publisher of the year award 2021, and has been featured on the Emmy Award winning show Red Table Talk.

Jamie loves to laugh, spend quality time with her adult daughter and family.

Editor in Chief Bald Life Magazine
info@baldlifemagazine.com
www.alopeciasupportgroup.org
www.Baldlifemagazine.com

Introduction

❧ • ☙

Michele Irby Johnson, Visionary
Speaker | Trainer | Consultant | Coach | Entrepreneur
Published Author | Talk Show Host | Pastor

As little girls, our parents painstakingly ensured that we looked presentable from our heads to our toes. Every hair was in place with coordinated bows, ribbons, and clacking colored balls that accessorized our outfit for the day. As we come into our own, we grow into our authentic selves experimenting with our personal look – sometimes we stand out and other times we blend in with the crowd by wearing the latest trending style. At some point, our hair makes its own decision, and it chooses to "go its own way" or some medical issue has robbed us of our glorious locks. In *My Bald is Beautiful,* brave sisters of all walks of life share their stories of hair loss and they encourage others to embrace their new, bold look, without shame.

❧ • ☙

"MY BALDNESS EXPOSED MY BOLDNESS"
Michele Irby Johnson

As indicated in the introduction, I was one of those little girls that always had my hair done. My mother did not play that leaving out of the house with our hair all over our heads. Why? Because it represented her... her parenting. My mother came from a time where the parents were criticized if the children came to school or were out in public looking disheveled, unkept, or uncared for. Although my mother worked nights, she made sure that her girls were properly groomed before she sent us out into the world. I recall one time when we had picture day and I went to school adorned in dress that my mother had chosen. I felt so pretty. I took my school photo as scheduled, but when those photos came to my mother, she was livid...simply beside herself when she saw that I failed to brush the edges of my back hair back after I got dressed. It was customary to cover our heads at night to "preserve" our hairdo, but somewhere between getting up and getting out of the door, I missed this minor detail, and it has been forever captured in my third-grade photo (I can see my mother's face right now).

From this moment forward, I understood the importance of appearance – particularly my hair. I became almost obsessed with making sure that my hair was always in place and presentable to the world and so that it was pleasing to my mother. Even as I grew up and was "in charge" of my own hair style choices, I was still meticulous in my hair's appearance. Constantly asking questions like: *"Is it good in the back?" "How's my flip?" "How's my mushroom?" "Are the curls good or did they fall?" "Is my relaxer still holding up?" "How are my edges?"* It became a silent, ongoing battle within me to make sure that not one hair fell out of place. Quite frankly, it was rather exhausting.

Coming of age as a young woman, I would often admire the beautiful hair of other women of color (no offense to any other race – but I acknowledged their beauty from my cultural perspective that I could intimately relate to). I often commented on how thick, curly, bouncy my 'sistas' hair was. I would dream of having such beautiful locks. My hair was what I like to call 'confused and temperamental.' Because of my biological background, I had a number of textures in my hair – all of which gave me the blues with styling choices because I wasn't sure "who" was going to show up on my head each day. With ancestors from many points of Africa, Ireland, Europe, and Native Indian, my hair had a personality of its own. If I wore it long, I fought with it. If I wore it mid-length, I fought with it. If I wore it short, I fought with it. My daily battle became *'What am I supposed to do with this hair?'*

I remember when I started paying for my hair to be styled at the hairdresser. I would seek to emulate those styles of women of color that I saw on television or in the movies…the bob, the snatch-back, the asymmetrical, the Anita Baker or Halle Berry, the Clair Huxtable, and the like. With each attempt at capturing a style that I *thought* would suit me, I realized that because of my hair type none of these styles lasted more than a day. I was often discouraged because every two weeks I would spend what I considered an exorbitant amount of money on a hairstyle that only lasted until I woke up the next day. You see, my hair was soft, fine, curly in some places, and "native" in other places. Like I said before, my hair was confused, and it frustrated me every day. On those days after I spent $85 or more for a hairstyle and awoke to a flattened style, I would brush it back, bump it with a curling iron to give it structure, or simply put it in a dancer's bun if it was long enough to do so.

With every attempt to beautify and tame this hair of mine, it failed and so I thought I had failed. I recall sitting in one of my stylists' chair one evening, and she said to me, "Your hair is thinner in the top than anywhere else. Did you notice this?" I told her that I thought it was just one of those crazy ancestral textures showing up. She said, "Your hair follicles are less concentrated in the crown of your head, but it is not really noticeable to the average person and doesn't appear to be of any concern." I was like, "As long as it doesn't show, I'm fine with it." Little did I know that this was the start of what I ultimately discovered in 2019.

Fast forward through my adult life, my hair chronicles did not improve one bit. I vacillated between braids (although not too tight because I was extremely tender headed), updo's, roller sets, traditional locks and sisterlocks…and of course, my dancer's bun! From time to time when I became fed up with my hair, I would do the big chop, but afterwards I would be horrified at how I looked with a TWA (tiny-weenie-afro). I thought (in my own mind) that I looked like a boy with breasts, so I fell into wearing wigs. This was the worst season in my life because I was having hot flashes early in my 40's and my head would sweat profusely, and face would shine like I just ran a marathon. I could not wait to get home and snatch that "girl" off (I called her *'Flossy'*). Over time, I would let my hair grow out long enough for braids, but soon noticed for myself that the area in the top of my head had wider spaces than the rest of my head and I resorted to my typical move – pull that hair up to cover it up.

In 2014, I nixed the braids, and I became more comfortable with the short hairdo when I did the big chop again and colored it to a beautiful bronzy auburn. It was sassy and sexy! Most importantly, it was easy and carefree…a little gel or activator and I was out of the door and ready to take on the world. One day, I noticed that the top of my head had become REALLY thin. I could touch my scalp. Why was this spot so bare? I tried to grow my hair longer in the center so I could *"palm curl"* over the spot, but it became more difficult to conceal. Once again, I allowed my hair to grow out long enough for braids and then eventually long enough for me to pull my hair up into a ponytail and attach a *wiglet*. Yes! This was a good look. No one knew what was going on under that hairpiece. No one knew the struggle that I faced each morning trying to hide the ever-increasingly large bald spot in the top of my head.

My self-esteem started to tank at this point! I felt like I was lying to the world, to my friends, co-workers, and family. That is not to say it was their business or their battle, but I always felt as though someone knew that I was hiding something. I became paranoid – although the average person would have never known it. One day while I was leading a small group at church, we were reading the book *Do It Afraid* by Joyce Meyer. It was a small book, but it packed a powerful punch. In our discussion, I asked the ladies what was their greatest fear – what was holding them back from doing what they wanted to do, who they were called to do or to become? Each presented their answer with some reluctance, but they shared openly. When they asked me – the leader – the same question, I swallowed deeply, and I shared with them my 'secret' struggle. They were surprised – each exclaiming, "We can't tell!" I was relieved that they couldn't tell, but now they knew why I had started wearing this little hairpiece. One of the sisters said, "You should just go bald! It would look great on you!" I was appalled at the suggestion, and I was like, "Oh, No... That will NEVER happen!" The sister offered that I pray about it and consider it for my own personal liberation in spite of my fear and apprehension.

By this time, I had visited the Veteran's Medical Center in Washington, DC to see a dermatologist to find out what was going on with my hair. I was informed that I had alopecia. To be exact, I was diagnosed with Central Centrifugal Cicatricial Alopecia

(CCCA), which according to my doctor occurs in most African American women and results in permanent hair loss in the crown of the head and spreads to a greater portion of the scalp. When my doctor confirmed my diagnosis, I was stunned. I was speechless. I was ashamed. She suggested topical solutions, vitamins, and a free customized wig (retail price $1,000). I tried the solutions, the vitamins, and was even fitted for the wig, but never went to pick it up because I was not about to be trapped inside of a wig (that's my personal choice). I asked her if there was a chance that my hair would ever grow back and she said as a matter of fact, "Unfortunately, it will not grow back!" I was hurt. What was I going to do now? The wiglet wasn't holding anymore. I didn't want to keep using creams and vitamins that the doctor KNEW would not help but would "make me feel better" about my condition. I threw all of those senseless "remedies" in the trash and took a deep breath about my next steps.

In 2019, I was attending the Homegoing Celebration (others call it a funeral) of a faithful, sainted church member. The Spirit was moving through the service and true to form, I "got happy" lifting my hands and throwing my head back in an exuberant praise. Something happened that took me right out of my praise. I felt a slight breeze on the top of my head. What in the world? Wouldn't you know it, my wiglet had disengaged itself from the 10 bobby pins that was holding it in place. Oh, my God…I almost lost it! My secret was about to be exposed. I discreetly *adjusted* my wiglet and *maintained my cool* for the rest of the service. That would have been so embarrassing if it had fallen off in the middle of a praise (Father, please forgive my moment of vanity – LOL).

As I was leaving that service, the Holy Spirit chastened me saying, "You allowed your fear and pride to stop you from praising God – over a hairpiece?" I was upset with myself and cried the rest of the way home. A few days later – after I had recovered from what could have been a fiasco – I was sharing what had happened with my then fiancé. I also told him what the sister said in the small group. To my surprise, he agreed! I was like, "What? You want me to be bald?" His response, "You're beautiful no matter what!" This is where you all say, "Awwwwwwwww…" but I digress. At that moment, I asked him to bring his clippers and to cut my hair. Now mind you, he had never seen me without my wiglet… I had only shared with him that I had alopecia.

At this point in my journey, the entire center of my head down to my ears was bald. I only had hair from about an inch above my ears and around the back of my head (picture Benjamin Franklin or Bozo the Clown). I admit it was getting more difficult to pin the wiglet on because there wasn't anything in the top of my head for the bobby pins to attach to. So, my future hubby showed up at my condo, clippers in hand and he placed a chair in the center of my kitchen. I slowly and fearfully removed my wiglet – revealing to my hubby-to-be what I was hiding. He may deny it, but I could see the shock in his eyes. I began to tear up and he comforted me and told me, "Everything will be just fine. I've got you. I'm not going anywhere."

On June 3, 2019, my fiancé freed me of the secret of my condition. He used the clippers to cut what remained of my hair and then he used a five-blade razor to shave me clean. He wouldn't let me see myself until he was done. To my surprise, when I saw myself, I wept. I was actually pleased with what I saw. I felt life return to my spirit. I could now see me. I wasn't focused on how to camouflage, hide, or cover up my progressing condition. Rather than my condition controlling me…I now took control of my condition. I was now bald, and it was the most liberating feeling.

The next day was Sunday and I had to go to church. As I got dressed for service, I beat my face and put on something stylish. I stood in the mirror, and I looked at the woman that was looking back at me and I felt revived, rejuvenated, BOLD! I waked into the church and every head turned. The members were like, "Elder Michele… You look amazing… You are rocking that look…!" My confidence went through the roof. They were more excited about my look than I could have ever imagined. The sister who suggested that I go bald was elated and exclaimed, "You are so beautiful!" When the Pastor saw me, he asked, "What is this a new fashion statement?" to which I responded, I was losing my hair, so I made a bold choice to let it all go… to be fiercely BALD and BOLD. He couldn't say anything after that proclamation!

Since going bald, I have found that a new me has emerged! I feel like I can conquer the world uninhibited, unencumbered, unapologetically. I no longer feel that I have to fit the mold of the world's standards of beauty or femininity. Bald and bold has become my new existence. Things I did before were amped up in my baldness. I *did it afraid*, but now I had more courage than I ever thought I could. Yes, I was a woman of God, preacher, teacher, author, entrepreneur, singer, dancer, an educator, a speaker… Yes, all of those things, but NOW, my fierceness was on fleek (as the young people say). I never really thought I was as pretty as the other women… I always saw myself as average, a plain Jane, if you will. But when I embraced my baldness, I started walking in the scripture Psalm 139:14, *"I will praise thee; for I am fearfully and wonderfully made: marvellous are thy works; and that my soul knoweth right well* (KJV). Now, I can own that Word from God because now I believe it with all of my heart. I am no longer disguising myself so that I can feel like I am loved and accepted. I am no longer secretly competing for the accolades or the approval of others. I love ME! I accept ME! I approve of ME!

For those of you who may be struggling with walking in your authenticity…embracing the beautiful person that God created you to be, I want to encourage you to stand up and be counted. Hair loss is just a thing! It is not YOU! Your hair is not what makes you beautiful, accepted, smart, loved, wanted, or successful. It's just hair! All that you are comes from within – from your spirit, your soul – where God has shaped you in His perfect image. So, be counted among the BOLD! Be counted among the BALD! Be counted among the BEAUTIFUL! You are more than your fashion. You are more than your accessories. Continue to remind yourself and shut the mouths of the naysayers, the gawkers, the critics and shout *"My BALD is beautiful! I am more than my hair!"*

Bold and Beautiful…

Michele Irby Johnson

BALD IS NOT A HAIRSTYLE...IT'S A LIFESTYLE

Cʒ • ʓↃ

Lisa D. Barnes

Let me start by saying, *hair doesn't make you who you are.* I want to encourage every woman to embrace their own hair process and learn to rock any hairstyle you choose, even if your choice is being bald and beautiful.

I have had several female family members that went bald due to cancer/chemo and survived it all. Praise God! However, I did not realize I automatically associated seeing a bald woman with some type of sickness. It was just a given for me. I don't know why that was the case, when my mom has been a bald woman since 2004. She is not sick (thank God); it's just hair loss that is hereditary on her paternal side. I believe I didn't associate my mom with being "bald" because she wears a lot of wigs, hats, and scarves. However, being the Queen that she is, when she does wear her bald head, she rocks it every time!

The decision of becoming a bold, bald, and beautiful woman was a process for me. It was not a hard one, so to speak, but a calculated one. It all began with the decision to get locs on December 10, 2010. I knew I had to be committed to growing my locs from the beginning. I knew it would be a lengthy process to say the least. I was nervous about going through the "ugly" phase of growing locs. Going through the transition of going from using relaxers to natural hair and then from natural hair to locs can all be a bit intimidating. In that transition, I had to get the relaxed hair cut off (which was about four inches). This big chop made my starter locs look even shorter (the baby dreads). I quickly learned to embrace the growing process and have fun with it. I made sure my makeup and earrings were on point whenever I stepped out. I wanted to give the total package at all times. I must say during my process, the only regret I had with making the lifestyle change of getting locs is not starting them sooner.

In embracing my process of growing my locs, I studied maintenance tips and styling techniques via YouTube. I learned to start locs on other family members and even started locs on my granddaughter's hair. I loved every minute of being loc'd until I became ill in 2017. I was going through menopause and having hormone issues during this illness as well, all of which can be a strain on your hair, which was the case for me. I was diagnosed with an autoimmune disease. I was then prescribed a medication which had chemo in it (with the side effect of hair loss). I had my locs for seven years by this time and they were hanging down passed my thighs. They were very long and healthy and red (I love vibrant colors). I did notice over time while on the medication my edges started thinning to the point that my locs looked like they were attached to string, which was the hair around my edges. I did this for almost two years until I had no other choice but to make a decision about cutting my locs off.

I have worn short hair styles in the past, but I always had some type of bang to cover my forehead. It took two years to commit to a decision about cutting my hair because of childhood emotional scars. I was a very petite child with a big head and a lot of long thick hair. I got teased a lot about my forehead growing up, so I wasn't sure if I was ready to totally expose myself to the cruelty again, especially in the age of social media. That was my hesitation, but I finally gave myself "the talk:" I am an adult now, I wear makeup now, and my head is in proportion to my body now. The opinions of others concerning the size of my head is their business, not mine. So, if you find yourself second guessing a decision or being hesitant in making a decision concerning your hair, just remember, if I can go bald you can, too. Be encouraged.

I was turning 50 years old in October 2019. I made the decision to cut my locs for my 50th birthday. However, that plan changed Memorial Day weekend in 2019. I traveled to Detroit to spend time with my best friend. I purposely packed plenty of scarves and headbands for my trip. I happened to see a picture of myself during this trip where I was without a headband or scarf…in public. I don't know what happened, did I forget the headband? Scarf? or did I just decide not to wear anything at that particular activity? The picture was a side view and from that angle and distance it looked like I did not have any hair from ear to ear and then my locs started. In my mind, I felt like other people looked at me and saw the Genie from Wil Smith's movie "Aladdin" (it had just been released that same month). I had my locs in a long ponytail just like the Genie in the movie, too.

After that trip, I made the decision to cut my locks immediately. I could not wait until my 50th birthday. That Friday, May 31, 2019, I was at the barber shop getting my locs cut off. I didn't go bald at that time, just cut my hair very low. This was a new phase on my hair journey! Of course, I colored my hair red, and I embraced my new look. My thinning edges (no edges) were still very noticeable even with the short hair style. My edges were still not growing and was not blending with the rest of my hair. However, I rocked my haircut the best I could.

Since I cut my locs in May, instead of for my 50th birthday, I decided to get my hair cut very low for my 50th birthday party. It was almost cut bald then leaving just enough for me to color my hair…red. It was a cute cut, and I received a lot of compliments from men and woman alike. However, you could still see how my edges were not there or blending with the rest of my hair. I let my hair grow some and wore a short curly afro for another year.

I cut my hair almost bald right before my 51st birthday photo shoot. That is when I received the phone call. In September of 2020 a bald, bold, and beautiful young lady in the community reached out to me to invite me to a photo shoot for bald women. I was honored to be invited, but I let her know I was not bald. She understood and still extended the invitation to me. After that conversation and completing the photo shoot for my 51st birthday, I decided to go BALD. In that decision, it was like a weight was lifted off me. I felt free and liberated in that moment. I gained strength in my decision. I gained victory in my decision. At times, I felt I was not walking in confidence when I was going through my transition phase of losing my locs. I regained my confidence. My walk became stronger. I stood taller in my decision to go bald.

Now that I was completely bald, I accepted the invitation. I attended the photo shoot for "bold, bald, and beautiful women." I found my people! It was like I was inducted into a whole new world. The love shown, the unity, the respect, the encouragement given and shown during the photo shoot was phenomenal. It did not matter how your journey started…what it took to get there, we all arrived at the same destination at the same time.

The consensus of that group of ladies was boldness, confidence, love, respect, spice, resilience, triumph, and unity! I was there for all of it. The group poses and individual poses were remarkable. It showed me that hair does not make you who you are. These ladies were giving fashion model vibes including myself. It was a wonderful experience. We were able to share some of our hair journey with each other that bonded us for life. Some were indeed bald due to sickness and disease, some due to alopecia, some just made a simple choice to go bald. Every story was unique and different just like the different head shapes and skin tones. A rainbow of love and flavor!

I am still bald and loving it. I get compliments all the time. I have even been told I have the perfect head shape to be bald. Hmmm, imagine that! Everywhere I go, men, and women (women with long hair, women that wear weaves, women that wear wigs and other bald beautiful women) give compliments freely. I get more compliments than I do insults. If there are any insults or ridicule, I don't hear them, per se. Now, I do get the occasional looks and stares from children when they see my bald head and my face mask (due to COVID-19) while walking in the grocery store because they think I am sick…The same response I gave to bald women when I was child, I'm sure. I feel that I represent a whole new awareness for bald women everywhere. I'm loving it! I embrace it! I wear my makeup and my jewelry. I make sure I'm stylish when I walk out the house. I make sure my head is always shaved or presentable. Just like I did with my locs. I have embraced being bald. I just want to encourage other women that are hesitant about making the decision to go bald or the decision was placed in your lap due to illness…Just go for it! Whatever your journey is, embrace it, rock it, be bold, be beautiful, and remember being bald is not a hairstyle, it's a lifestyle! My bald is beautiful, yours can be, too!

LISA D. BARNES, M.S., STUDENT BCBA, RBT

Lisa D. Barnes is the author of her first book *What Now: How to Survive a Loss Due to Suicide*. She grew up in Kansas City, Missouri, where she spent her early years learning how to cook and bake under her great-grandmother, Big Ma. Lisa relocated to Savannah, Georgia in 2007. Lisa is a hard worker and loves, loves, loves her family. Lisa raised three sons and is the grandmother to eighteen grandchildren. Lisa continues to share her love for children by working professionally as a registered behavior technician (RBT) with autistic children, as a behavior aid for foster children and as a service coordinator for developmentally delayed babies (birth to three years of age).

Lisa loves helping others. Lisa is currently serving as the chapter journalist/historian of the Nu Chapter of Iota Phi Lambda Sorority,

Inc. She is an entrepreneur of her own businesses: Barnes Consulting and Exceptional Services, LLC and Connected with French Property Management. Lisa writes early in the morning, then spends as much time as she can spoiling her Yorkie puppy (Paisley) and Beagle Mix puppy (Piper).

To reach Lisa to give encouragement or for appearances, please don't hesitate to contact her at (912) 631-1657 or by email at lbarnes1969@gmail.com.

BALD BOSS

CR • 80

Michele Zaret

She had long, thick, luscious locks. She was the only one of her sisters who was obsessed with doing her hair. She would spend an hour in the mornings blow drying and flat ironing and styling her hair.

That was up until September 2004. Before going back to college at the age of 21, I went to my hairdresser, and he told me that I had a quarter sized bald spot in the back of my head. I knew it was alopecia and I knew what I had to do. When I was a child, my sister had a bald spot, and I went with her and my mom to the dermatologist where she got something injected into her head and her hair grew back and she never had another problem. So, once I got home, I looked up a dermatologist and made an appointment.

I never liked going to the doctor. I have what is termed as "white-coat anxiety." Going to a dermatologist for the first time wasn't any different. After I filled out the forms, I sat patiently, palms sweating, wondering what was going to happen and if it would hurt? Once my name was called and I got into the room, the gentle demeanor of the doctor started to put me at ease. We discussed alopecia and what it was: an autoimmune disease where my white blood cells attack the hair follicles and causes the hair to

11

fall out. We talked about the different types of alopecia: Alopecia Areata, Totalis, and Universalis and that it would be unlikely that I would lose all of my hair. We then discussed the treatment: cortisone injections into the bald spot. So, I flipped my head over, showed her the spot and she pricked my scalp with maybe five little pricks. It didn't hurt very much, and the appointment was done. She told me to call back if I'm not seeing any results.

My hair grew back, and I went back to college to finish up my last semester. That was a very stressful semester as I was graduating a semester early. I got engaged to my boyfriend and was trying to figure out what to do once I had my bachelor's degree in Math. I ended up with another bald spot. When I went home for Thanksgiving, I made another appointment with the same dermatologist. Same routine. A couple little pricks and I was done. The hair grew back in a couple of weeks.

Once I graduated college, I moved back home with my father and started working for a company in New Jersey through a temp agency. It wasn't exactly what I had in mind, so I decided to apply for graduate school to become a teacher. I was accepted into a program and worked during the day and took classes at night. Again, my stress levels started to increase. My life at home with my father was not very pleasant and both of my sisters lived far away. Things were also rocky with my fiancée and by July of 2005 we had called off the engagement but stayed together and tried to make things work. My bald spots started to grow in size and numbers, making my trips to the dermatologist more frequent. We also experimented with other treatments: Rogaine, a course of Prednisone – an immunosuppressant drug, and this tar-like substance that was awful…none of that worked. The injections worked to grow my hair back, but it didn't prevent my hair from falling out in other areas. Every time I took a shower, huge clumps of hair would come out. It was very upsetting.

My second year of graduate school in 2006, I moved in with my boyfriend into the house he built, and we were engaged again. Newly living with someone proved to be harder than I thought, and my stress increased. By the spring of 2007 while I was student teaching, my bald spots were getting more and more difficult to hide. I started wearing wide head bands to hide the giant spot at the top of my scalp. One day when I was teaching, a student asked me why I always wore headbands. It was mortifying, but I just told her it was because I liked them.

I finished graduate school and got my teaching license, but I realized that teaching wasn't for me. Unfortunately, you don't really find that out until you actually do it. Thankfully the company I was working for offered me my full-time position back and I have been with them ever since.

Life at home wasn't getting much better. My fiancée and I were fighting all the time. We would break up, I would move out, we would get back together, I would move back in. This went on for a couple of years. I kept getting more spots and kept going to the dermatologist every 4-6 weeks. By 2008, I started wearing wigs. I didn't really know anything about wigs, so I just bought a cheap synthetic one online that looked close to my natural hair color and style. Wigs can get very expensive and human hair wigs range anywhere from $400 to $4,000. That was definitely something I couldn't afford, but the synthetic ones weren't bad.

In the spring of 2010, I went to the dermatologist for another round of shots. I started counting how many injections I was getting. Now *that* appointment was painful. With my next appointment I talked to the doctor, and we decided to stop treatment; it wasn't working anymore. New hair wasn't growing, there were too many injections and I noticed that my eyebrows and eyelashes started falling out. Oh, no! This was turning into one of the other alopecia disorders.

I kept wearing my wigs and I had very little hair left. The hair I did have left turned very brittle and so one fateful evening I drank a bottle of wine and asked my boyfriend to shave my head for me. That was very traumatic, and I sobbed over the death of my hair. I never let anyone see me bald except for him. I would visit my sisters and I would only take my wig off when I went to bed. I would wear makeup every day, eyeliner since I had no eyelashes left and I would draw my eyebrows on, even just to walk out to the mailbox.

14

In October 2010, I moved out of my ex's house for the last time. I moved to a town closer to work and was renting a one-bedroom apartment in a house. I was starting to have fun with my wigs. I would get different ones in different styles and colors. The nice thing about synthetic wigs is that they come pre-styled and even after washing them the style would go right back to how it was. They would last about six months with daily wear, and I would spend between $40 and $120 on them.

I ended up going to Washington, DC for a conference for the National Alopecia Areata Foundation (NAAF) – a foundation that provides support and does research for Alopecia – with my sisters and their husbands. There were bald people of all ages: a bunch of little kids running around that were losing their hair to adults that just lost their hair. I learned that there was very little research done on it, but they were mapping it with the human genome (I gave a DNA sample to help) and they found it was linked with other autoimmune diseases like Lupus, Multiple Sclerosis, and type 1 Diabetes. I met people like me whose hair fell out gradually and I met others where they went completely bald within a matter of days. It was a very eye-opening and educational experience and I felt so lucky that my family was there with me.

When I decided to start dating again, I wasn't sure what to do. Do I tell the guy that I'm bald and wear wigs or don't tell him? At first, I decided not to tell them. I was doing online dating and all of my pictures were of me wearing wigs and my makeup was all done up. One guy touched my hair and could feel the weft of the wig; I told him I had extensions. The first time I stayed at a guy's house I made sure to tape the wig down. The next morning when I went into the bathroom, I only had one eyebrow and I didn't have my makeup on me! I quickly shifted my hair over that eye, gathered my things and said I had an appointment to get to. I never made the mistake of not carrying eyeliner and eyebrow pencil with me ever again.

Eventually I started to tell the guys that I wore wigs. Some cared, some didn't. Almost all of them asked if I was sick and I would have to explain what alopecia was. I decided to go to cosmetology school at night in 2011. When I started, I was wearing black wigs. Then on a Monday I showed up with a platinum blonde wig. The only person that asked if it was a wig was my instructor and I said, "Yes, it is, but the black hair was a wig, too." During the course of my time at cosmetology school, I was able to educate others on the different types of hair loss and alopecia. On the day of my graduation, I put together a "Bald is Beautiful" fundraiser where we did $10 blowouts, and all of the proceeds went to NAAF. I believe we raised around $1,500.

Once I received my cosmetology license, I started to volunteer with the Look Good Feel Better Foundation. This foundation helped cancer patients with skin care, makeup application, and taking care of wigs. I had to go into Manhattan for training for a day and then I volunteered at a local hospital. Unfortunately, the classes weren't offered for very long at the local hospital and I stopped volunteering, but it was a great experience, and it has made me think about starting my own non-profit for women with hair loss regardless of the cause.

In 2012, my sister became pregnant with my niece. When I found that out, I knew I wanted to be a good role model for her, so I decided to start going out without a wig to teach her that just because someone looks different, doesn't mean that they're bad or scary. My very first time I went out bald, I was with my sister, and we just ran errands on a sunny day. I was so self-conscious, even just sitting at the carwash, but hey, it was a first step.

I started to get more and more comfortable going out bald, but I always wore a wig to work. Everyone in the office knew I wore wigs, but my coworkers in the warehouse didn't really speak English and I didn't know how they would react. I got many different reactions. Sometimes people would stop me on the street and ask if they could give me a hug. Sometimes children stared and made rude comments. But, more often than not, I would get compliments on how beautiful I was…and I was starting to believe it.

In 2017, I decided I wanted to get my head tattooed. Because of the healing process of tattoos, I knew I wouldn't be able to wear wigs anymore. So, a week or so before my appointment, I went to work without a wig for the very first time. Again, very self-conscious, but guess what? Nothing happened! No one said a single thing or acted any differently towards me. The tattoo I got was of a lotus flower because they are something beautiful that grows out of darkness and that felt like me. I get compliments on it all the time.

Now, I never wear wigs except for Halloween or if I'm doing something fun. In truth, they're not very comfortable. They're itchy and they get really hot, especially in the summer. In the winter, I'm always wearing a hat though and I have a bunch of really cute ones. I belong to many online alopecia support groups and have even gone to alopecia events: dinners with other Alopecians, Fundraisers, etc. I even carry cards on me that explains what alopecia is and I'm always open to explaining it to others that don't know. And guess what? There are a lot of guys that like my bald head and don't judge me.

To those of you that may be struggling with hair loss, please know that you are not alone. There are a lot of inspiring women who are bald, and even more celebrities and athletes are coming out about their hair loss. So, I encourage you to embrace yourself for whoever you are and however you look because it is not about what is on the outside that counts, but who you are on the inside. So don't be scared about other people's judgments – that makes them ugly even if they are the most physically beautiful person on the outside. Stand tall, be proud, and most of all, be YOU! You are not your hair, and you, too, are beautiful.

MICHELE ZARET

Michele Zaret has a bachelor's degree in mathematics with a minor in writing. She is a Supply Chain Manager in the fastener industry. She also has her cosmetology license and freelances as a hair and makeup artist. She used to volunteer with the Look Good Feel Better Foundation that helped cancer patients with skincare, makeup, and wigs.

The youngest of three girls, she has lived most of her life in Hudson Valley, New York. She belongs to and contributes to many Alopecia support groups. Feel free to reach out to her at mzaret02@yahoo.com.

My Bald Is Beautiful: I Am Not My Hair

BALD BY CANCER

CB•ED

Arlene McGuire

My journey to being bald began on April 25, 2018 and ended February 2020. One of the ways I feel better about this life changing event is that I now understand that we can help each other with the truth about our specific journey and survival…Journeys through illness, losses, and other heart-wrenching situations of life. Journeys of joy are easy, of course, and everyone is delighted to listen to those. However, telling of a journey into darkness is a bit foreboding, and mostly shunned. Over the years, we have found a great healing from telling of the dark side we traversed. Mostly because the responses have been received with a little less trepidation. I am thankful for that, because that whole new mind set will allow me to tell you where and how I have made this journey. Needless to say, I am overjoyed to do so. My love to those who fought, fight, and survived! To my Grand Mother who may have had this very same cancer and succumbed to it in 1995. To my mother who walked through with such grace, I cry even now as I see her bowed form before me. She walked right through it, with the knowledge that the God she loved with all her mind, soul and spirit walked with her, in the darkest of days.

This may be one of the many books such as this you have

bought…or the only one…either way I hope to impress upon you how strong you are. I hope to plant the seed of faith of the power you have within you. Please accept my offering of faith in you that any journey you are on, will be thwarted by belief in yourself.

In 2004 My Mother's Cancer Journey began and she stayed cancer free until 2012. She was admitted to the hospital, she had other health related issues, exacerbated by the cancer. After five months, she was removed from life support on December 29, 2012. We were both diagnosed with the same very rare cancer, Hodgkin's Lymphoma. Her sites were internal. Hodgkin's Lymphoma Extra Nodal presented outside my body. Mine was an external site on my forehead, and it had an addition to its' name: Large Diffuse B Cell Lymphoma, Hodgkin's Extra Nodal Lymphoma. Now you know, I thought I was just so very important having a cancer with such an impressive name. LOL!!!!!!!!! Well, I got over that real fast!! The Oncologist who treated me was the same one that treated my mother.

My Cancer Journey

When the horror called cancer came home to roost in my body, the sound of those words made me feel frozen in time. The world as I knew it ceased to exist. A resounding NO shattered my brain. 2…3…4…5…snap out of it!!!!!! "Breath before you asphyxiate" someone, somewhere said, and I complied. Moving in slow motion I collapsed into my car. The journey had begun. Moving to consultation and planning where a very dismal picture of my life began to unfold. The feeling that all my hopes, dreams, desires, and aspirations were dashed. All I could see was a number that would represent the rest of my days. A choking feeling was automatically in effect when I contemplated that I had, maybe 10 years at the outset to exist. The bile rises, dry heaves come to the forefront, that wave passes in its own time. I recover and try to recall what I was doing before that shut down. Yeah, now I can laugh at those occurrences. I refer to them as being spaced out, which was the reference or colloquialism for being very high back in the day. Over time, those episodes faded, and I began to accept my status of cancer

A patient at age 64. I have often wondered if my mother felt these awful moments at age 74 when she embarked upon the position of cancer patient. I spent that year assisting mother through her chemotherapy treatments and all other doctor appointments. I recall how exhausted she was upon our return home. Now I know how she felt. Mostly she simply wanted to lay in her bed, to just get through that treatment. I must admit that is exactly what I did as well. As the months wore on and my body wore down, I promise you the only thing I knew to help myself was to pray. So many times, I went into those requests for strength; I knew in my spirit that that is exactly what she would do…what she did. I humbly approached the Mercy seat and stated my request!!

These past months have tested my faith…brought me to my

knees from sometimes blinding pain and discomfort. Some days it was so very dark at noonday, with a head that was so foggy. There was no light in my heart or in my mind. The nights were just a continuation of the dark days. Soul searching, unbelief, doubt, copious tears, uncontrolled laughter wreak havoc with my mental state. Through it all, my spirit asked one thing of me…that I keep reaching for the Hem of His Garment…simply because I am not alone. He has had to carry me for a bit, but I do a jig on the good days and remain thankful for His grace and mercy with each and every new day I now receive.

After the shock about this absolute disaster of a diagnosis, I had to summon all the strength I possibly could to stand up straight. It felt as if the punch to the stomach took my breath, and I could only bend over to gasp for air. Each new day I would struggle to find the power to stand. But stand I did; I stand today and am able to look back and say, "I was made better by cancer."

So, to begin at the beginning, of the journey: A lump began appearing on my forehead, it was very painful. My Primary Care doctor suggested I see a Neurologist. A CT scan was done on my head, it showed that I was having silent migraine headaches for quite some time. So, steroids were prescribed to treat the pain and swelling, while the symptoms I presented with were deciphered. It seemed I had three different things from the symptoms I had. So, a series of medications began to eliminate them all and get to the correct diagnosis. After a year, the lump continued to swell the left side of my head and it was so painful. I was referred to a Dermatologist; the first one had no idea what to do and promptly referred me to a surgeon. An exam and biopsy were done. That test took almost four weeks before I received the results.

So, finally on the 25th of April the call came and with it was the referral to an Oncologist. Imagine my amazement and joy when I heard the doctor's name. It was the same doctor that treated my mother. She was now going to be tasked with treating me. I had the same type of cancer, except that it manifested completely differently from the way my mother's did. Hodgkin's Lymphoma attacks the lymph nodes. My affected presentation of cancer cell growth happened only on the side of my head. I recall now how unnerving it was to see the few strands of grey hair that began growing right there. I began to feel that it made me look distinguished over time. When I think back now, it may have been my forewarning of trouble ahead. I thought it was only in the area of where the grey had started growing, that always became swollen.

Post-chemotherapy, I was sent for radiation treatment weeks. When the protective masks were attached to my head, two areas were isolated for the radiation treatment. I had the same Hodgkin's Lymphoma, but mine had the additional designation of Extra Nodal. Meaning it manifested outside of the body. Where mother's only attacked Lymph nodes inside her body…under arms, groin, throat.

25

Well, I was happy about the fact that mine was just in one area. I was not happy that it disfigured me. When attacks happened, I could not even look in the mirror because my face became so swollen, twisted, distended, distorting my facial features. Then the blinding pain was never far behind. So, I now had some idea of how much pain my mother had experienced inside her body.

The next step was the Pet Scan to investigate my body for any other locations that may have been infected. There were none. Next, I would learn of the type of chemotherapy and radiation treatment that I would need, as well as the meds to begin the process of killing this cancer on my head. My Husband saw me through this entire ordeal. He would schedule his days off from work to accommodate my treatments. So, I always felt secure.

As you read this, I want to say to you that as trying and as difficult as this process was, I found a quiet understanding about my mortality. If this illness was to be my vehicle home, then so be it. That late in life it becomes clear that new beginning awaits you. I had a very close call to prove it. My blood volume fell very low once during treatment, but I asked to go home instead of being taken to the hospital. I promised to get to the Emergency Room the next day if I had not overcome the fatigue. Well, I did not, and I promptly drove myself to the hospital that next morning, after my husband had gone to work. Upon arrival, I was immediately put into a bed and the request for the on-call Oncologist went out. They immediately administered blood to save my life.

As you wait for that event to take hold, you realize before you pass out that, maybe just, maybe you do not get to come back. Maybe this is your moment to move from the terrestrial into your celestial. Allow me to be overly dramatic right here!!! I truly felt death was not to be feared…not embraced per se, but maybe it could present a feeling of quietude as opposed to fear and trepidation. My heart spoke in those moments and reminded me that *I had done all I should have, and departure is preparation not termination.*

I have had continued blessings in my life after two years of remission: The first is being bald. I just shave and go. So much pressure removed from my life. Regarding this benefit, I must say a bit more. During my mother's treatment, I shaved my head to help her see how she would look if she lost her hair because of the chemicals. We favored each other so much. She did feel more comfortable after that. Her hair got wispy, but there was no balding. I grew my hair out and went on to being a blonde, which was so vastly different, but I enjoyed the change. When my turn at hair loss started during radiation, I simply shaved it off. The areas that were radiated would not grow back. It made the choice easy having embraced the bald idea because it helped my mom and made it doubly easy to embrace for the rest of my life.

I am still amazed when folks stare and sometimes people will even ask if I am bald because of cancer. I then adopted the phrase *"bald by cancer"* as my response, even if not asked. It gives a unique feeling of the survival of the fittest mind set. I have gone through, and I am on the other side of such a trying illness. I am thankful each day I look at my head without any hair and think that I am blessed. Blessed with another day, week, month year and more to come.

Now, back to the other cancer benefits: Secondly, I now have a budding hobby that is burgeoning into a small business. I am building an artwork legacy for my grands and great grands. There are so many pieces in my collection that everyone will get several pieces for their own space. Thirdly, being on short time causes you to truly enjoy the minor things of life more than you previously did. Short time by man's count as the blink of HIS EYE is 1000 years to God. I could be here for a real long time if that's the case LOL!!!! What I mean by minor things is that, now a walk in my backyard is uplifting. Being able to stare at a full moon is a satisfying experience. Buying day old flowers and roses at the market is a sweet-smelling savor of dying. A sip of water during the night and a 'thank you' whispered for still being alive is a smile to put you back to sleep. I really enjoy seeing the grands and great grands on Facetime or on videos. They have such busy schedules that I am fortunate to get such calls. LOL!! So, in my mind as age comes up and my recovery continues, I enjoy the simple things much more. When complicated events arrive, I do my level best to go easy. I must say I am not always successful with that behavior, however. LOL!!!

Please indulge my words of encouragement in this moment. On the days when I still need encouragement to move forward, my reflection in a mirror reminds me that my celestial awaits my becoming a new creature of His likeness. This beautiful body will be at rest. No matter what difficulties await you in the near or distant future, hope will see you through. When the darkest hours come upon you, hope allows you to stand strong in your belief that the best is yet to come. The despair that may be your daily life today will be more tolerable as, the hope you have as treasures is stored up in your heart. It is the place your Father looks at and knows everything there is to know about you. It is here that HE seeks your requests and provides the answers you need. It does not always coincide with what you think you want. You may have to do some work to see the manifestation of your desire. However, it is always the exact answer that you should have. HE IS NEVER WRONG!!

I thank you for your time to read this. I do hope you have found something you can recall...Something to lift your spirit from my story!!! To the gentlemen who read this, embracing the new bald being you now have before you should be exciting. I would ask you to find new ways to let that lady know of the beauty you have seen in her all this time. Impress upon her that she is even more beautiful, because the tender touch you apply to her head does so much for you. Need I say more??? To all the ladies who read this, my encouraging words to you would be: When you look in the mirror, see a creation of great beauty…not by the standards of mankind, but by a loving Creator.

Would your earthly father be saddened if he knew you thought you were ugly? What would your mother think if she knew you thought the same thing about your looks? Would your Heavenly Father feel the same pain as your earthly father and mother? Begin today to find the beauty in each of the features of your face. Today admire your own body and accept that it is perfection. You can sustain it with good habits so it will last through old age. See yourself in your world, aspiring to greatness, achieving, accomplishing goals, and growing. Strive to be just YOU…You are BEAUTIFUL!!!

If hair loss becomes a part of your life, you will simply see another side of your beauty, the addition of which now makes you unique and outstanding. Also, your Heavenly Father has already approved your shaved head in His Word. If we must be bald, there is no disgrace, and we can cover it for practicality. Living without a cover brings so much attention, and it does take getting used to. The opinions and judgments of those around you should matter very little! This is a new transformation that is yours alone. When you embrace it whole-heartedly, it makes it much easier to see your beautiful new self.

You are *not* your hair! You are so much more in HIS sight. Those who seek to know you will do so from the light in your eyes, and not only from your outer form and beauty. **My bald is beautiful and so is yours**!

ARLENE MCGUIRE

Arlene McGuire is a Hodgkin's Lymphoma Extra Nodal Cancer survivor as of 2019 and she found doing artwork to be her daily lifeline during Chemo and Radiation Therapy. Her hobby, post retirement, became the mainstay that enabled her to keep her spirit elevated during treatment. She remains thankful for the support of her husband, children, and grandchildren throughout that journey. Arlene's artwork is created using acrylic paint, alcohol ink, oils on stretched canvas and Yupo Paper.

She is presently doing dedicated purpose driven artwork. Funds received will assist her daughter with Physical and Occupational Therapy treatment and equipment. She survived a Stroke last year and has returned home in need of therapy. ALL sales will be used for the care her daughter needs. Arlene also contributes to St. Jude Hospital for Children and Feeding the Hungry.

Publications on Amazon: *Hanging Out In The Quiet*, *Beyond The Moon*

Compilations Essays: *Dear Depression, Reflections On Purpose, Women Of Faith*, and *My Bald Is Beautiful: I am Not My Hair*.

My Voice Over Imaging work can be heard on The Urban Sound Suite with DJ Matt Houston. Weekly shows on Mixcloud.

Business: https://www.instagram.com/avamacart/

Website: arlenemcguire.com

Facebook: arlene.mcguire4

TikTok: ArleneMcGuire723 Haiku Poetry Readings

Contact: mcguirearlene384@gamail

BALD, BEAUTIFUL, AND BLESSED

ᨠ•ᨡ

Yummekia Boggon

My journey with alopecia started when I was about 19 years old, I am 44 now so it's been well over 20 years! It was tragic for me because I was getting these bald spots and I had no clue what was going on. My mom is bald, and I had no idea why. As kids, we heard so many stories as to why she was bald, not one story ever came from my mom; she never talked about her baldness. She always wore wigs and she even slept in her wigs never taking them off, at least not in front of anyone. Until this day, my mom and I have never had a conversation about her baldness, but I think after she reads this book, I will have the conversation with her.

I was still living in Tennessee and my hair continued to come out in patches. I had enough hair to where I could wear it in styles that would cover my bald spots. I could even slick it down in a back ponytail to cover the spots up. I remember one day while I was pumping gas and I had a bob style haircut; it was very windy on this particular day as I was standing there just pumping away all of a sudden, a gust of wind blew my hair back and oh, Lord, it uncovered my bald spots!!! I don't know if anyone saw it, but I was so embarrassed. Having those bald spots didn't really bother me because I never thought my hair would come out all over. I came to the conclusion that I would just wear hairstyles that would just cover those spots. I was so wrong! After that hair blowing in the wind incident, I decided to go to a doctor to see what was going on? Why was I losing my hair? I had no clue about alopecia and still didn't after I left the doctor. He told me that it was bad nerves that was causing my hair loss. The doctor said he could stick my bald scalp with needles to try to stimulate the hair growth, I quickly declined. I said, "I'd rather be bald than go through that pain. I have zero tolerance for pain."

Life went on with me covering my bald spots with different hairstyles. I never talked about my bald spots. In November 2003, I and my three kids moved to South Carolina; this is where I met my wonderful husband some years later. Before I met my husband, he knew that he was going to marry a beautiful bald lady! My husband and I met on my space. Yes, I said MySpace!

I drove to meet the man that I fell in love with through two weeks of conversation and the rest is history! Not long after we met, I decided to show him my balding head. By this time, I had a flawless routine. If I didn't have a 27-piece weave, I had a short-styled wig and I could work wonders with a scarf or bandanna! Well, I told him that I had something to show him. My nerves were all in my stomach, but I knew that I needed to show him because at this point, he still didn't know about my balding head. As I grabbed the scarf to reveal my head, I whispered *Lord I can't believe I'm showing this man my balding head!* To my surprise, my husband was like, "Girl, that ain't nothing. You are beautiful with or without hair!" He went on to say, "You might as well cut that little bit off!" I did cut it off eventually, but I still wore my wigs, sometimes my 27-pieces and of course those scarfs and bandannas!

Remember when I said my husband knew that he was going to marry a bald and beautiful lady? After I finally revealed my balding head to him, he said a little while back he watched an episode of the Tyra Banks show, which featured a group of bald women telling their stories and he said, "I would marry a bald lady." So, here I am bald, beautiful, and blessed married and to my wonderful husband for almost 13 years. God is so good and doing just what He promised me!

As life went on, I still wore my wigs, my hats, and my scarfs because I was really ashamed to show my ball head. I only went to the salon for a 27-piece or a quick weave for special occasions or events. The stylist would always ask me if I wanted them to cover my head with a towel, and I would always say *yes*! Being young and bald was tough for me. Even after my husband told me that I was beautiful with or without hair, I was still ashamed and uncomfortable. My husband and I had to start taking our younger children to a dermatologist for their skin; we decided to ask the doctor to look at my head to determine what was going on? Why was I losing my hair like this? At that time, I still didn't know anything about alopecia.

I didn't know that alopecia was my problem until that day. My reaction was unexplainable, and I asked why in the world is this happening to me? This doctor told me and my husband that I could get the treatment of the needles being stuck in my scalp to try and stimulate the hair growth. We both said no at the same time! My husband said to the doctor, "I'll buy my wife any kind of hairstyle she wants. She's not going through that" and I couldn't agree more! No tolerance for pain y'all – LOL – but I gave birth seven times, but that's another story!!!

I found out what type of alopecia I have when I did a research paper in school. I decided to do it on alopecia. My alopecia caused me to lose all of my body hair. I researched which one causes you to lose all of your body hair, and I found it to be Alopecia Universalis. I still wore my wigs, my hats, and my scarfs but it did not bother me as much. I was slowly getting comfortable with my beautiful baldness. As time went on, more people in my family started seeing my baldness. I am reminded of a time when I was at church and my wig came off while I was being prayed for and I was so involved in the Spirit of God, the lady was trying to put my wig back on my head and I threw it across the floor! Oh, I am out of my shell now! God has a way of getting you out of your comfort zone in order to be an example for others through your testimony!

And so, the baldness boldness began! I would go to Bible study on Tuesday nights without anything on my head or if we had church meetings, I would wear hats and you could see the perimeter of my head showing some of my baldness. My husband told me to go bald. He said, "You are beautiful, and it fits you!" He said, "You have the perfect shaped head." Just about everybody says *I have the perfect shaped head!* Our Apostle said the same thing about my beautiful bald head. She was one that helped me along the way! I can now go anywhere bald with nothing on my head. The first store I went to showing off my baldness was the same grocery store that I worked at for years prior; and we live in a small town, so everybody knows everybody. I can remember that particular day in the store without anything on my head; I wore a pink shirt, so the people were probably thinking I was going through chemo or something. I felt all eyes on me, but not one person said anything. I was so nervous, but I was okay. After that day, I began to go out more and more with my beautiful baldness!!!

Stepping out in my BALD BOLDNESS has open doors for me to converse with people about baldness, encouraging them to just do it! My baldness is truly an icebreaker. Women are stopping to ask questions and talking about their baldness. I had a lady pull up beside me and say, "You gave me the courage to embrace my baldness," and this alone makes it all worth it! Now, I can understand the blessing of being bald and beautiful because I can use my situation as a ministry tool to help someone that's feeling ashamed and low in spirit to understand that they are *fearfully and wonderfully made!*

I have no problem with being bald and beautiful. I prefer not to wear wigs as much now. As a matter of fact, these days I'm in wigs way less – LOL – they are just too hot for me now! I get so many compliments about my beautiful bald head. One that really stands out happened recently while I was waiting for my husband to finish with Physical Therapy. I was sitting in the van looking at my phone; I had the windows down and usually I don't because it gets so hot. The Lord knows what to do and when to do it. I was feeling a little down and I heard a voice say, "hey, you!" I looked up; it was a lady that stopped to tell me that I was beautiful, and she said, "remember that always." That really put the biggest smile on my face! I said, "thank, you Ma'am" and I said thank you God because that was all God. He knew I needed that!!!

I'm living my truth. I am a bald black woman and guess what – LOL – I don't have to worry about getting my hair wet in the shower! I don't have to worry about shaving anywhere on my body. So, thank you Alopecia Universalis for this beautiful baldness of mine!

I was a shy person, but now I am bold! If you are going through this ordeal, trust and believe once you release yourself from that bondage – free yourself – you will be just fine! There is a place for us out here in this world. God has got us, and we have a bunch of bald, bold, and beautiful bestie's all over this world! So, free yourself! We are here for you! I'M LIVING MY TRUTH… I'M BALD, BEAUTIFUL and BLESSED!

YUMMEKIA BOGGON

Yummekia Boggon is BALD, BEAUTIFUL, BLESSED and she's living her truth! Yummekia was born and raised in the great state of Tennessee, but South Carolina has been her home for the last 18 years. South Carolina is where she met her husband of 12 years, Elder William Boggon. They have seven beautiful children and five amazing grandchildren.

Yummekia absolutely loves the Lord with all her heart. She loves to bake her delicious treats from scratch pound cakes; she is the BALD BAKER! She loves people, she's a giver at heart and will help any and everyone that she can. Her family means the world to her; she loves them all in a very special way!

She's an upcoming author with two best sellers in the works: The first, *Letters of My Life*, her true-life story, which will be an inspiration to all women who have made bad choices in life and how

God will heal the wounds of those bad choices. The second work God gave to her in 2020 when her husband went through some health challenges that landed him in a wheelchair. This book is entitled, *Marriage Ain't For The Weak.* This catapulted her into being her husband's 24 hour 7-days- a-week caregiver, which consists of being a nurse, a physical therapist, a social worker, a chauffeur, etc.! But she absolutely loves taking great care of her husband! She's BALD, BEAUTIFUL, BLESSED and she's living her truth!

Contact Information:
Yummekia Boggon
yummekiaboggon@yahoo.com
(843) 372-4978

CHOOSING TO OWN IT!

☙ • ❧

Annie J. Mewborn

"Do you know you're going bald on the top of your head?" That's what my hairstylist said to me one afternoon as I was sitting in her chair for my regular weave touch-up. My heart sank. I was dealing with this "bad hair" issue once again. Over the past three years, I worked with my stylist to see if she could treat my hair, getting it to grow. Even after moving from New Jersey to Maryland for a new job, I never missed an appointment, taking the 3-hour drive faithfully to get my hair done. So that day, when she told me that I was going bald, I didn't even know how to react. I just always had very thin hair. It didn't grow very fast, and I just thought of it as something hereditary, passed down to me by my paternal side of the family.

I've always had issues with my hair for most of my life and just couldn't seem to find peace with it, which made me very insecure and self-conscious about my appearance. Even in the Army, my hair was very thin, so I learned to cope and embrace short hairstyles. Chile, I had finger waves, the "Anita Baker" haircut, keeping the sides and back closely tapered to mask the growing thinness. Over the years, I learned to embrace short hair, and quite honestly, I loved the freedom that came with it. I was wearing my hair in such a way

45

that I tried not to concern myself with it, thinking, "Okay, I'm just gonna deal with it." However, I knew deep down; it was all a lie.

Later, the weave craze came, and I was hooked! I would drive to Baltimore, and then it was Philadelphia, and then came the micro braids craze! I can recall sitting up in a chair with three African women working on my hair from 6 a.m. until sometimes ten hours later. I've had micro braids, box braids, etc., etc., yadda, yadda, yadda. In retrospect, throughout my "hair journey," I was festering this self-inflicted pain on my hair, never realizing that years later, there would be a price to pay.

Fast forward ten years later, and the obsession with my hair (or lack thereof) grew beyond my control. Paranoia set in deep, and I was obsessed with no one except my closest confidants who knew the truth about my hair issues. The turning point came when I took the extensions out of my hair and stood in the shower while shampooing my hair. I felt my hair in my hand, and it was coming out in clumps. Mortified, I dried and combed it through as best I could, and when looking in the mirror, I saw that I looked like Bozo the Clown. For those of you who don't know what Bozo the Clown seems like, he doesn't have any hair in the center of his head, only on both sides – yeah, that's the image I saw. I literally broke down and cried. After those tears, guess what your girl did? Yep, I went right back to gluing those tracks on my head and kept it moving. But in all honesty, it was at that point I knew I had to seek professional advice regarding my hair loss.

Finally, I got up the courage to make an appointment with a dermatologist, which resulted in a terrible experience. In the examination room, the nurse asked me to remove a portion of my hair weave before seeing the dermatologist, to make it easier to assess my situation. Upon entering the room, the doctor took one look at my scalp and, in a matter-of-fact tone, flatly stated, "You have alopecia." While I looked at him with this surprised look on my face, my thoughts were like, "For real? This is what my twenty-dollar co-pay paid for?" He continued, "Your hair follicles are damaged – they're not going to grow back." There it was – my prognosis. I was dumbfounded. I sat looking at him with his mouth moving and continuing with this contrived spiel about how his office could perform a biopsy and for me to make an appointment with his staff. Ten minutes was all it took, then the dermatologist pivoted and left the room. Needless to say, on that note, THAT dermatologist never saw me again. Continuing to wear weaves became my routine for several more years.

Fast forward to 2018, I had the fortune of going to teach abroad in Abu Dhabi, the United Arab Emirates. In preparation for moving to another country, one of the things that was definitely on my mind was, "How am I going to be able to get my hair done in the Middle East?" In other words, how was I going to live with this lie? Was my truth or my "tell" going to be discovered if I couldn't find a way to buy hair weave anywhere over there? So, I loaded up my suitcase with ALL my products – glue, needles for sew-ins, and bags of hair. Luckily, some stylists could do my hair when I arrived, so my "secret" was safe.

While in the UAE, I had the opportunity to meet this beautiful Sista with a bald head, Kimberly Carey, and meeting her became the turning point in my life. She was a model, a teacher, and just all-around fierce! Unbeknownst to her, Kim became my muse, and I longed for the day that I could walk in confidence with my baldness as she exuded. Kim was hosting a breast cancer fundraiser, so I jumped at the opportunity to meet her in person. It did not go well. To start, the makeup artist assigned to do my face made me look horrendous, in my opinion. Feeling as if everyone's eyes were on me, I just felt mortified, and I sat in that chair, wanting the ordeal to be over. Kimberly, seeing my discomfort, tried to reassure me. Listening to my concerns, Kim was very understanding and stated, "I don't know what you see because we're not looking at the same thing. I think you look gorgeous." Yeah, right. Respectfully disagreeing with her, I went ahead and took my pictures, did my little video clip, and beelined it to my car. Back at my apartment, I washed all the makeup off my face and cried. I missed my opportunity to meet Kim, having been excited at the thought.

Looking back, I believe my reaction to the situation was another episode of my low self-esteem issues, and I didn't handle it properly.

A few days later, I got a call from Kim, and she told me that I'd won some of the door prizes that were raffled off at the fundraiser, and she wished to meet to give them to me. This became the defining moment in my bald journey. Kimberly shared her own story of her alopecia journey and how she came to terms with being bald. While I don't want to tell her story, I truly believe that Kim's sharing of her testimony gave me some sage words of advice about living with alopecia. She told me, "If this is something that you really wanted to do (shave my head/go bald), then you cannot be a shrinking violet. You must own it! You've got to walk in the confidence that you know who you are, with or without hair. Only you know when you're ready, but when you are, I'm confident that you will make the decision." Wow, I was left with a lot to think about when Kim left, so I did a lot of praying, and I did a lot of crying. But in the end, my decision was made.

On November 18, 2018, I shaved it all off. What I saw in the mirror was another person, and it stunned me because I had no idea just how stunning I looked. And yet, afraid to show my baldness, I began wearing turbans and head wraps (still hiding) till one of my Emirati students asked me if I was converting to Islam. "No, sweetie, I am not."

In the UAE, religious services are held on Fridays. Per my weekly routine, I awoke Friday morning – getting up super early because my intent was wrapping up my head – however, God had other plans. My fingers became all thumbs, and that day for the life of me, I could not get my hands to work properly to wear a headwrap. Frustrated and about to give up going to church, I heard a voice on the inside of my spirit, saying, "Do you trust me?" The voice repeated, "Do you trust me? I loudly replied, "Yes Lord, I trust You!" So, I got dressed, put on my makeup, oiled my scalp, grabbed my purse, and headed to church. Parking in the lot, nerves set in, and I silently said a prayer. Just as I'm walking towards the church entrance, a lady from South Africa abruptly stops me and gasps, "Oh my God, Sister, you are absolutely beautiful!" My mouth dropped open, and I burst into tears. Shocked, the woman looks at me and asks what's wrong. I told her that I knew this was God through tears because I was so nervous about walking into that church and revealing my baldness. After sharing a hug and hearing the sister's reassuring words, I walked into the sanctuary with my head held high and my spirit lifted. Feeling rejuvenated, upon arriving home, I posted my first pictures of being bald and shared my testimony with my Facebook family. Responses and direct messages came from all over. There was such an outpouring of love, support, and encouragement from so many people that it was overwhelming and confirmation that my choice to trust in God had been the right one.

Choosing to go bald for almost three years now, I'd love to say that it has been an easy journey, but it hasn't. Quite frankly, there are occasions when I long to have hair, but then having hair has never been the *real* issue. There are so many social and cultural constructs that exist around women and hair...beauty, femininity, sexuality, and cultural expression, to name a few. I can vividly recall Kim's candid warning of what awaited me when I decided to go bald. She said, "You are going to find out that not everyone is going to be in agreement with your decision, but it's YOUR decision." No truer words were spoken, having experienced side-eye glances and occasional smirks from onlookers who have no idea how living with alopecia feels. I've had inquiries from "concerned" folk who wondered whether I had cancer or why I didn't choose to wear a wig after shaving my head. Because women, in particular, are branded by their hair in a world centered on an unrealistic image of beauty, I've observed that these inquiries offer greater comfort to individuals who ask them. People are uncomfortable with those who have alopecia and choose to become bald since it disrupts the status quo in areas they don't understand. That isn't my concern!

Living with alopecia every day is a trial and an adventure, I'd love to say that it has been an easy one, but it hasn't. Every day is a pilgrimage, a challenge, but I feel God's transformative process is happening – changing me – changing those around me. After struggling with alopecia for years, when I made the decision to go bald, I said to myself, "I'm tired of hiding, and I don't want to hide anymore." Now, to quote my friend, Kim Carey, I OWN IT – the beauty and the boldness of being bald and the freedom that is given me; I've often asked myself this question, "Annie, what took you so long?" Discovering the true beauty in embracing who I am and who God has made me to be, I've lost count of the number of people I've shared my testimony with, just as Kim shared hers with me. This alopecia journey has been one of the most significant turning points in my life, and I continue to trust God every day. I am praying for the confidence and strength to encourage and empower the thousands of women struggling to live a life with alopecia so that they, too, may experience freedom.

ANNIE J. MEWBORN

Annie J. Mewborn is an educator, activist, Gulf War veteran, domestic abuse survivor, lay speaker, writer, mother, and grandmother. She is a published writer with her articles and devotionals appearing in online magazine articles such as The NextStep Magazine, Recruiter Journal, and a piece titled, *Meditations on Motherhood* featured in the 2004 anthology titled *Motherhood Memories: Stories of Hope, Joy & Encouragement.*

Formally the 2016 Teacher of the Year for Talbot County, Maryland, Annie has taught internationally and in the United States, and is currently working as a secondary English teacher, committed to fostering relationships and positively impacting the lives of her students. She has earned a Bachelor of Science in Business Management from Thomas Edison State University, a Master's in Education from Western Governors University. She is an active doctoral student with the American College of Education. Annie seeks to empower others and continues to use her God-given talents to mentor, coach, and allow herself to be a living testimony to inspire others.

For speaking invitations, encouragement, and questions, Annie can be reached at transformativegrace@outlook.com.

I AM

℃ • ℈

LaQuisha L. Jackson

I've always been told that the greatest sentence comes after the two words, I AM…Growing up, light-skinned with long hair was the "thing!" As a woman of color, it was embedded in me through family and society that my hair had to be passed my shoulders and straight. This "model" somehow was going to ensure that not only would I become successful in life, but I'd also be "blessed" in the relationship area. Hair was the definition of who I was supposed to be. I, to the world, was my hair, but to me, I had no clue who I was.

For as long as I could remember, I used to have dreams about looking a certain way. Even though this look in my mind did not align with the look of the world, it was who I wanted to be. My mother wasn't big on allowing me to cut my hair, so for years ponytails, weaves, and relaxers were my life! My mother used to tell me that back in the 70s, the man or woman with the biggest Afro was considered to be "that stuff!" He or she was the one everyone else envied. We evolved from the biggest and boldest hair to the longest and the straightest. But what about US *in between* folk, rather, nonexistent. I've heard so many people, to this day, degrade or look down on women who choose to have short hair. The ugly questions of "why would you cut your hair" or "are you sick?" The premature mind of so many, kept them in a box of ignorance to think that every woman with short hair was either sick, depressed over some man, or going through something in life. Having short hair was never seen in the positive light that it should have. As for me and my crown, I didn't know it then, but I needed my hair to be gone.

I desired to be different. I craved to be this woman with NO HAIR who was still seen as a force to be reckoned with. Powerful, desirable, bold, and definitely beautiful. Stories of the strength acquired from our hair are deep seated and rooted in history of our black people. There's a Bible story of a man named Sampson. It was believed that his strength came from his long thick locs of hair. He, in fact, was untouchable until the night his hair was removed from his crown! Imagine being taught that your hair is what controls your very being. Not only does it control your existence, but it is the pure source of your strength and without it, you are nothing. Accompanied with this story, believers felt that the longer the hair, the easier for YAH (GOD) to reach down and pull one up to the heavens when it was their time to leave the earth. Contrary to popular belief, I can't imagine YAH (GOD) denying me at the gates because my brush cut and luxurious waves on my crown are not to His liking.

It took me years to not only get out of my own head but to finally kick unwanted people, thoughts, and feelings out as well. I have become Sampson 2.0! A Woman totally opposite the stories told in the Bible. The strength gained from removing my hair is monumental. Yes, I still spend some time in the salon chair but not in unwanted hours. No more competing for the beautician's attention while she completes five heads at once, leaving my scalp to fend for itself as the creamy crack chemicals penetrate my very existence, leaving me in a headspace of fire. No more broken edges from the Africans braiding not just my hair, but also somehow catching my personality in the process. If you know, you know! I gained an extra 30-45 minutes, maybe even a whole hour of sleep not having to get up and try to curl or master the perfect ponytail. This negative "look" that most can't accept has formed nothing but positive energy within my being.

I had no idea what shape my head had or how I would look once I chose to relinquish the creamy crack saga. How do you prepare yourself to respond to a world that is already full of negativity? One thing I've come to realize is that "in a world of negativity, I am the positive." Stripping my crown of the loose long strands that sat upon it for over 30 years, was the best decision I've ever made for my hair and my life. For me, being bald is more than bold and beautiful, it is FREEING! Why did it take me this long to become the woman that I wanted to be? Why did I allow the thoughts, feelings, and opinions from others to dictate who I am and who I've been called to be? Television and social media acted as catalyst in my world of self-doubt and low self-esteem issues. When Beyonce hit the scene, I

57

knew 100% that I would never be the woman that the world sees as perfect! I am perfectly imperfect, and I am okay with that. Mediocrity is my middle name.

Maintaining this image that was pleasing to the world was causing my more disruption than peace in my life. Trying to come up with money, styles, and time to keep my appearance a certain way, ended up causing more depression than pleasure. I still ask myself as a woman "who is bald headed by choice?" Why did I give the world and my hair so much power over my life? I recall cutting my hair and having men tell me, "You shouldn't have done that," or the unnecessary and unwanted comments about looking too masculine. It didn't help that I'm very into the gym and aware of my physique. It took me a lot of time, prayer, and meditation to fight the physical demons that stood before me on a daily basis to go against the very thing I had longed for since I was a little girl.

My brother, God rest his soul, played a major part, both good and bad surrounding the type of esteem I had within myself. For years I was his "little ugly." Not one time did he give me a positive compliment or help to make me feel beautiful. He, too, was big on long hair; I mean he hated short hair on women with a passion. When he was murdered on 9/11/2020, I had a TWA. For those too young to know, a TWA is a teeny weenie afro. I wasted $300 in hair for his funeral because I knew he wouldn't want me there looking like that. The day after his burial, I took that $300 weave down and paid another $50 to have my hair cut off and dyed. The courage that he gave me in his death and departure, even from the other side, was so strong. I felt for years I had been someone everyone else wanted me to be. I maintained a look that was satisfying to the world and the least bit satisfying to me. I admired my brother my entire life for his carefree, nonchalant, 'all about me' attitude. These three traits that he embodied were now mine. His death brought a fire out in me that I didn't even know I had. For so many years I was searching for someone inside me that I would never find. Instead of being who the world wanted me to be, I finally became the woman I needed to be for myself and my children.

As the clippers ran across my scalp and each piece of strand fell from my head, it was as if I were releasing every trial and tribulation I had gone through in my life. I embraced not just the baldness in my scalp, but the transgressions and pain that were festering and brewing deep down in my soul. Things I had not been aware of or cared to acknowledge, somehow, I gained the strength to face them and take control over every piece of my life. Unlike Sampson, my hair was weighing me down. Understanding energy and the universe, this made so much sense. Throughout the years, through everything I had gone through, my crown carried that spilled over energy into everything I had done moving forward. The narrative needed to be rewritten. The confidence that spilled from my pores moments after the completion of my new hairdo, illuminated the entire place. The blonde added to my crown was just the icing on the cake. See not everyone can "rock" short hair and do you know the main reason why that is? It is because it truly is a CONFIDENCE thing.

Do you know how strong, bold, and how fierce a woman you are to walk around with a short hair do. I love my short hair, or as some would say, "no hair" look because it accentuates every feature that I possess as a black woman. There is no hiding the wideness in my forehead or the elongation of my neck. Be it my eyes, nose, or my voluptuous lips, you notice ME! My hair took away from what I could even see. My focus transitioned from the world to myself. I am in love with being able to work out or get in the shower with no worries. The heat and humidity in the summertime are the least of my worries. Rain? Who needs to dodge rain drops anymore? Not me! I see myself from a whole different point of view now. And who would have thought that by removing my hair, I'd become the happiest I've been in my life on top of successful.

This day and age, the crown of a black woman has undergone so much scrutiny. What is considered professional and what is not. So long as our hair was long and straight, we were okay. When we introduced the "ethnicity" to the workplace, it was like dropping a bomb over Bagdad. To see a black woman with either an afro or no hair at all was a culture shock for some. For me, cutting my hair not only boosted my esteem, but also my business. Taking that step to be different from everyone else gave me the courage to do what I had dreamed of doing for so long, which was truly launch my business and teach young African American females about anxiety, depression, other mental health disparities and positive self-esteem and body image. So many young women, like myself, go dang near a lifetime struggling with our appearance because of the societal factors and the lack of education surrounding self-love, self-care, motivation, and mental health awareness. I never realized how much I didn't know about who I was until I became bald.

If you are a woman struggling to make that choice to transition over to the "Bald and Free" side, as I like to call it, let me slightly encourage and persuade you into why you should join us. Hair, for one, in fact is dead. Why spend so much time, money, and energy into dead things. Hair or no hair, you are still you. Wonderfully and perfectly imperfectly made. Made in the image of Kings and Queens. Your CROWN – unaltered – is more beautiful than you realize. Don't allow people, things, or places to keep you from being the woman you have been called to be. If you have a desire to be without hair, follow your heart. If having hair has been something you've had all your life and you've recently began to lose it for whatever the reason, know and understand that hair does not make you who you are. Hair does not determine your next chapter in your life and hair should not be an element that determines your happiness. Always seek to see the positive light in every situation because it does exist. The one thing that also gave me the strength to cut my hair and keep it off, was the fact that it's just hair and as long as I have LIFE, that's all that really matters!

LAQUISHA L. JACKSON

LaQuisha La Chelle Jackson, RN-BSN, "Coach Q" is a proud mother of three, a disabled veteran, cancer/domestic violence survivor, Mental Health and Wellness advocate/mentor, published author, blogger, Nurse Educator and Owner/Lead Mentor of HEART of TAY, LLC Youth Outreach for Girls.

She has published articles and been featured in *Ambition Magazine* and *Best Holistic Life Magazine*. Through the use of the 3 E's, LaQuisha seeks to Encourage, Empower and Educate young Queens to reach beyond their DIVINE EXISTENCE and LIVE and LOVE on PURPOSE. Her ultimate vision is to teach young black Queens to change their perspectives on self and life, one positive thought at a time.

She always reinforces to others that "What we do now, echoes in ETERNITY" ~ Marcus Aurelius.

To experience Coach Q's work and ministry, visit www.heartoftay.com.

I AM THE S.H.I.F.T.

☞ • ☜

Sheila Belle

My Journey: The Vision

When I was a child, I remember growing up in a large family house full of prayer, laughter,and love. My grandparents' house was the central meeting place for the family dinners, family games, and routine get togethers. In that same home, I remember the days of getting my hair washed and pressed by my mother. It was a regular routine and then on special occasions and for church I recall the fancy bangs and curly hairstyles. Hair just seemed normal to me; I had seen all lengths and textures, but I never personally added value to my hair. Then at the tender age of 13, I was introduced to Alopecia. My hair began to thin out and fall out every time I combed it, leaving behind small round bald spots throughout my scalp.

As a young teenager, I was not only shocked by what was happening but also shocked by the treatment from others, the quietness when I entered a room, the investigations of school authorities, and the many painful needle injections like nothing had happened and my world wasn't falling apart. I didn't understand fully what was happening and how Alopecia would invade my growth and my goals, but today I now believe a certain part of me stopped growing at that age. You see trauma has a way of shifting your growth and shattering your dreams. The one thing that stood out to me was the faith of my mother and her belief that my hair would soon return. Due to my mother washing, treating, and praying over my hair regularly, to my surprise within a year my hair began to grow stronger and longer. I began to dream again and believed I could fit in again and live a normal life that would include completing high school, moving on to college, getting a good job, marriage, a house, kids, and the white picket fence.

Fast forward seven years later, my second year of college the trauma I thought I left in the past reappeared and I lost all of my hair for the second time. Yes, I couldn't believe it…Alopecia strikes again. I was 20 years old, and my life began a downhill spiral; the stares began, the interrogation, the humiliation, dead-end relationships, and the onset of a 36-year bout of depression. Yes, on the outside it appeared that I was moving forward, however internally I was stuck! Why me? You see the *shift* happened without my permission.

My Shift: The Valley

The shift happened without my permission…I would go on to live the next 36-years of my life hiding in public. I remember as a teenager I had witnessed a neighbor live a hidden life due to alopecia. She chose to live behind her curtains and watch the games children on the street would play rather than getting in the game of her own life. I was determined not to be like her – I was not going to hide. I was going to live regardless; however, I came to realize that I was hiding from who God created me to be and I was hiding in public behind the wig. For so many years I never looked in the mirror without the wig. I didn't want to face the real me. I was hiding from the truth, hiding from depression and the shame. I started focusing on the wrong things to fill a void that felt like a hole in my heart.

There are too many experiences to mention that contributed to the negative thoughts that began to cloud my thinking and actions, which created my self-limiting beliefs. At times I felt ugly, not worthy, lonely, scared, defeated, embarrassed, not good enough, humiliated,unwanted, and stuck in my pain. These feelings resulted in me becoming a bad steward of my physical health, finances, and emotional health. Despite the challenges I have had to face, today I can look back and see how God kept me. Yes, there were many valley experiences, however I have been blessed to have many mountain-top experiences as well.

You see, I had not only spent thousands of dollars on my head in the form of wigs, weaves, and cover ups, I had also spent thousands of dollars on education, seminars, business investments, and personal development. I still had a dream to empower people to press pass the pain and become the best version of themselves, because in my mind that is what I was doing day by day. I focused on work and church activities, because the one thing that had been constant in my life was my desire to serve, help people, and worship. I believe my desire to serve and my private worship time with the Lord is what kept me going and gave me meaning.

The year 2020 came, and everyone was talking about vision, but I am not sure if anyone knew what was headed our way. It was the Covid-19 shut down. Yes, another shift! Life as we knew it shut it around the middle of March. We are a few weeks into the shut down and my birthday was approaching on April 4, 2020. I turned 55 years old quarantined alone and stuck. It was on that day it was impressed upon me to ***S.H.I.F.T On Purpose.*** I remember my prayer on that day was that during the mandatory shut down that the Lord would give me the strength to face my pain, seek the Lord and come out free to be me. ***This was my Exodus.***

My Exodus: The Value

Taking off the wig was my Exodus. When I took off the wig, I said goodbye to the old me and hello to the new me. I said goodbye to insecurity and hello to confidence…goodbye to low self-esteem and hello to self-worth…goodbye to procrastination and hello to purpose…goodbye to bondage and hello to freedom…goodbye to surviving and hello to thriving…goodbye to being overlooked and hello to standing out…goodbye to looking for love and hello to loving myself…goodbye to lack and hello to more than enough… goodbye to fear and hello to focus.

Today I am no longer living in the box. I realized I am the box! I am no longer bound, but free to be me; no longer suffering in silence but living out loud. I realized when you choose to look at a glass half empty, trauma has a way of stealing your voice, your life, your dreams, your strength, and your joy. However, if you choose to look at the glass half full, you will see that it was in the valley that you built strength, survival skills, character, passion, hope and purpose. Today, I am *hidden no more*, and I am walking in my calling as a Christian Life Coach. I am known as the B.A.L.D. Purpose Coach, B.A.L.D is an acronym for Bold, Authentic, Liberated Dream Coach.

If you are reading this book and feel you are letting your past determine how you live your today, if you are tired of feeling stuck, I just want to let you know that I know how you feel, and after years of tears, I found a way. I realized that the freedom I was chasing was all a mindset shift. Remember, God does not waste pain, and someone needs to hear your story. Your dreams and purpose are calling; will you answer? I got up and my prayer is that one day you will do the same.

My Prayer For You: The Victory

"[13] Brethren, I count not myself to have apprehended: but this one thing I do, forgetting thosethings which are behind, and reaching forth unto those things which are before, [14] I press toward the mark for the prize of the high calling of God in Christ Jesus." (Philippians 3:13-14 KJV)

You may not have lost your hair, but what did you lose that stopped you from dreaming, moving forward, and living your best life? My prayer for you is that one day you will ***Get Up! Shift on Purpose, Commit to the Shift, and Live the Shift*** by making a decision that it is time out for playing small in your life and hiding behind trauma experiences, whether they be emotional or physical. Face the pain, renew your mind, pray, and believe that in the end you win. Recognize you are more than your trauma, your failures, your disappointments, and any sickness. Make a decision to begin again and start your journey to getting rid of self-limiting beliefs. Say to yourself "Yes I can."

Seek Him In Faith For Transformation (S.H.I.F.T)

Breakthrough is on the other side of the shift. Kings and Queens come forth and speak to your shift. Say, **I AM THE SHIFT**! I am Strong. I am Healed. I am Inspired. I am Free and I am Transformed.

Remember the enemy came to kill, steal, and destroy your vision, your joy and purpose, but Jesus came to set you free.

SHEILA BELLE

Sheila Belle is a woman of God, entrepreneur, and transformational leader. Sheila is certified by P.C.C.C.A. as a Christian Life Coach. She is certified by John Maxwell as a Coach Speaker and Trainer, and she also has a certificate in Pastoral Counseling from Cairn University. She is a published author of *Don't Die In The Shift*, and her new published work is as a co-author in this collaboration entitled *My Bald is Beautiful, I am Not My Hair*.

Sheila's life scripture is Philippians 3:13-14. Her press is how she has been able to triumph over traumatic experiences in her life and to get free from her pain and walk in purpose. Understanding that to be truly free, she had to renew her mind from negative thoughts, self-limiting beliefs and accept that her journey of pain was her platform that would allow her to empower others to move from pain to power to purpose and shift from the inside out.

Sheila has a coaching program called She Got Up! that empowers women to say *Goodbye To The Old You & Hello To The New You* by using the acronym S.H.I.F.T. In addition, she speaks on Leadership Laws that empowers individuals to lead and live their best life. If you are ready to shift your life from the inside out, or need a Transformational Speaker, connect with Sheila:

Email: CoachSheila@aol.com

Website: ShiftwithSheila.com

My Bald Is Beautiful: I Am Not My Hair

I Give Myself Permission to Live

CRAFT

Carol Chisolm

Here I am in my early twenties and care-free. I had everything I could hope for, a great family, wonderful friends, and good health. A college graduate ready to take on the world. I had a promising career at an insurance company in the accounting department. Life was good. I had my own car, made my own money. I was strong, intelligent, and independent. There was nothing to hold me down. My future looked promising. I started dating an amazing guy who was an active-duty member in the Air Force. And it even got better when after a few months of dating, we decided to marry before he was reassigned to Germany. So off to Europe we left for an extended six-year honeymoon. We were world travelers visiting countries like England, Belgium, France, Luxembourg, Holland, and Austria. We even visited East Berlin before President Reagan demanded General Secretary of the Communist Party of the Soviet Union, Mikhail Gorbachev, to "tear down this wall." I was living a dream. How could I be so lucky? A wonderful husband, world travel, good health, etc. I was living my best life. What could possibly go wrong?

Two years after relocating to Germany, we had our first child. God blessed us with a 6-pound, 8-ounce healthy baby boy. God added this beautiful little person to our family. We were ecstatic.

Motherhood brought me so much joy. Moreover, I experienced the best hair of my life. Let me tell you, pregnancy hair is the best. Prenatal vitamins are to hair like Miracle-Gro is to plants. Talk about thick and lustrous, that was my crown, my covering. Because of the volume of hair on my head, there were not many styles I could not wear. Straight, curly, bangs, updo – I could wear them all. I opted for a Jheri Curl, which was popular in that day. I was so proud of my thick, shiny, wavy, hair. Then, the unthinkable happened. The gravest offense imaginable. A first-degree felony in the unwritten constitution of hair. The most serious of crimes committed in a society that places high value on outward appearance. Someone stole my hair. Someone or something. And like any common thief, it sneaked up on me without warning.

When my son was nine months old, we returned to the United States for a short visit to introduce him to my family and for a procedure to remove polyps from my vocal cords. It was time for a touch up for my Jheri Curl, so I visited a trusted friend's salon to have it done. Three weeks later, we returned to Europe, but we were not alone. To my dismay, the thief hitched a ride with us. I woke up one morning, removed my bonnet, and ran my fingers through my hair only to discover an unusual amount of hair in my hand. It was more than just the normal shedding. It was gobs and gobs of my hair. I jumped out of the bed and ran to the mirror. My heart raced with fear. "What is going on?" I screamed in horror. Wait a minute. This can't be happening. I must be dreaming. I grabbed my pick and began to comb through my curls only for more hair to fall on the bathroom counter. It was not a dream. It was a nightmare, but I was not asleep. Had it been a series of unfortunate events? Could it have been a side effect of the anesthesia from the polyp removal procedure? Could it have been the result of a chemical burn from the perm? Or could it have been a perfect storm of both events? I only knew that I had been robbed of my crown and glory, but at that time, I did not know who or what to blame.

For the next few years, I self-medicated trying every remedy I knew to restore my hair instead of reporting this crime to the authorities, i.e., a doctor or hair professional. I purchased the most expensive shampoos and conditioners. I wasted money on gadgets that claimed to massage the scalp and stimulate hair follicles. I even went as far as to do handstands against the wall. I was told when blood rushes to your head it would open the hair follicles. I tried every myth, fallacy, and old wives' tale I heard. If a charlatan came to town selling water as some miracle hair tonic, I would have been first in line. I was desperate. Then my desperation turned to despair. It was hopeless. My hair did not grow back. Instead, the hair bandit visited more frequently until there was no hair on top of my head. I could no longer disguise it. Why did it have to be like this? If I were doomed to suffer permanent hair loss, why couldn't it have fallen out along the nape, so I could more easily camouflage it? But there was no way to disguise it. I looked like Bozo the Clown, but even he had more hair than I.

For years, I lived in denial not wanting to believe I had been victimized by alopecia. Not only did it steal my hair, but it also hijacked my self-esteem, and took hostage my dignity. I was too afraid to report this crime to the proper authorities because I did not want to hear the "A" word. I already knew intuitively that this problem was greater than just the normal shedding of hair, but to even hear a dreadful diagnosis of the "A" word or allow it to roll off my lips meant sure death, the point of no return. The death of my hair growth. The demise of my crown. The assassination of my glory. The top and sides of my head were smoother than a baby's bottom. It was final. I accepted that my hair was gone forever but accepting it was not easy. It imprisoned my soul with fear until I became a co-conspirator in this crime. I became my own prosecutor, judge, and jury and sentenced myself to a life of fear and humiliation, convicted to a life of baldness. Shame became my prison cell.

I had no choice but to resort to wearing wigs to hide my shame. My wig acted like a correction officer governing every aspect of my life and supervising every activity. I would not be caught without my wig. If the doorbell rang, there was a mad dash to secure my wig on my head to answer the door. I am certain it was backwards a couple of times. I could not go to the mailbox or take my dog outside without my wig and forget about going down the slide at the water park with my children. That was not going to happen. I refuse to be featured in a video clip on social media's "shade room" with my wig floating beside me.

I condemned myself to a life of solitary confinement isolating myself from my family and friends. My shame was so grievous that I would not allow my husband to see me without my wig. My husband, my best friend, the person I trusted the most, the one with whom I had the most intimate relationship was not permitted to see me without my wig. I was too ashamed and embarrassed, so I isolated myself from him. I hated myself and the vision I saw when I looked in the mirror. How could he love me when I didn't love myself? How could he look at me and still see the beautiful, confident woman he married when all I saw was ugliness? Did he stay because of the kids? Did he pity me? I was not the nicest person or easiest to get along with during those years. They say misery loves company; well misery became my best friend, and we were in cahoots to make life intolerable so my husband could have a way out. He was intruding on my confinement. This was my cross to bear, not his, but no matter how I tried to isolate myself, he never stopped loving me or helping me bear my cross.

Wearing wigs made me feel as though I were perpetrating a fraud. I could vicariously be someone else by changing my hairstyles and hair color, but that was the "fake" Carol. I suffered from a case of mistaken identity pretending to be whoever I wanted to be when all I really wanted was to be the person God created. I wanted my own hair. Every time I'd come home with a new wig my husband would lovingly grab me and say, "Hey sexy lady." I would smile at him and giggle like a school-age girl, but that's the opposite of how I felt inwardly. I felt ugly, unwanted, and undesirable. My friends would remark, "I love that hairstyle on you." Or they would say, "You look great. You really have the face to wear wigs." If only they knew I had no choice in the matter. The alternative would have been repulsive. The wig made me look great on the outside, but they did not know the torment on the inside. I resented wearing those hot, itchy "rugs," but I was too afraid to face my reality. I began to pray not for my hair to grow back. I accepted that I would be confined to wearing wigs until God gave me a miracle. Instead, I prayed that God would get the glory in my life. God spoke to me and said, "How can I get glory when no one knows your struggle?" That was true. No one besides my family and a few trusted friends knew alopecia was the bandit that robbed me, not only of my hair, but of my self-worth. It was the stowaway that eluded me and stole my confidence. If no one knew my struggle, how would they believe that God performed an undeniable miracle when they saw me with a head full of my own hair?

These words changed my life forever. I knew exactly what God wanted me to do. I did not stop to try to process His request or understand why for fear of not going through with it. Just like when God told Abraham to sacrifice Isaac, he did not stop to reason. He believed God and trusted Him to provide a substitute (Genesis 22). It was settled. I had to get rid of my wig, walk in victory, and embrace my baldness. I went to the mirror and shaved the remaining pieces of hair on my head, and immediately I was set free, liberated from shame and humiliation. That burden of scurrying to find my wig just to answer the door was gone. Alopecia no longer ruled me. God exonerated me. He signed my pardon from a lifetime of fear and released me to a lifetime of purpose.

On May 2, 2019, I revealed my beautiful, bodacious, bald head to the world. I declared it my "re-born again" day. Now let me explain what I mean. Years ago, I accepted Jesus as my Lord and Savior. When I confessed, He saved me from sin and death. I was no longer a slave to sin, but then I allowed alopecia to become a merciless slave master and shackle me with fear. Because of this, I sentenced myself to a life of low self-esteem, self-hatred, shame, and humiliation. I suffered from an identity crisis, allowing my circumstances to define me. The scriptures say, *"Christ has set us free to live a free life. So, take your stand! Never again let anyone put a harness of slavery on you"* (Galatians 5:1, MSG). Now, I am determined to stand and to live victoriously.

The thief, Alopecia, disgraced me, but God honored me with a new life. In the words of my father, "Life isn't life unless it is lived with a divinely pronounced purpose," so I live. I live to bring hope to others who suffer in shame. I live to expose the lies from our past that we allow to be the truth of our present. I live to shine a light to uncover the darkness of our present that prevents us from moving into our future. I live to help others embrace their flaws and imperfections and to declare victory over their insecurities. I live to declare that I have alopecia, but it does not have me. I no longer run from my reality, but I live it out loud and unapologetically.

I am not my hair, and neither are you. Your hair is not the sum of your value. You are uniquely, fearfully, and wonderfully made by a God Who loves you unconditionally and judges your beauty based on the condition of your heart rather than your outward appearance. He has a divine purpose for your life, so don't allow society to impose their expectations of beauty on you. You are beautiful just the way you are, so begin to see yourself through His divine lens. Don't allow alopecia to bully you into a dungeon of despair and self-confinement. I encourage you to embrace those perfectly imperfect flaws – because everybody has them – and give yourself permission to live. "Life isn't life unless it is LIVED!"

CAROL CHISOLM

Carol Chisolm is an author, entrepreneur, singer, and songwriter with alopecia, an autoimmune disorder that results in hair loss. She is the host of "Onederfully Made," a weekly broadcast to inspire listeners to be courageous and confident in their own skin. She is a contributing author in the anthology, *She Writes for Him: Black Voices of Wisdom*. Her next literary work scheduled for release later this year is *Breaking the Shadows: How to Embrace Your True Self and Live in the Light of God's Glory*.

She coined the phrase ***"I have alopecia, but it doesn't have me"*** to remind her that we all are wonderfully made by God, and that our identity is in Christ and not a reflection in the mirror. She is passionate about encouraging people to find their purpose through music and the ministry of the Word and to break free from the shadows of bondage and walk in the light of His glory.

Carol has been married to her husband, Kim, for 34 years and they have two children and one grandchild.

To experience more of Carol's anointed ministry, visit her website at www.carolchisolm.com and watch her on YouTube at Carol Chisolm. You can also follow her on Facebook at Carol Chisolm Ministries and Instagram at @carolchisolmministries. You can email Carol directly for speaking and singing engagements at carolchisolmmusic@gmail.com.

MY HAIR...MY CHOICE

ɛʒ • ʓɔ

Stephanie White

I grew up in a house where my father owned a barber shop in our garage. Every Saturday afternoon, I'd watch countless men and women come in and out to get their haircut, trimmed, shaved, or just washed. I used to think, "I can't wait to get my hair cut" and sit in the big chair that could turn as if I was on a ride at Busch Gardens. My dad would tell me I was too young, but I knew the time would come. Just a few more years of pigtails and bows. While dad was in the barber shop on Saturday mornings, I was getting my hair done in the kitchen. Dad would walk in teasing me saying that it smelled like fried hair. Well, that's because, mom would have washed and pressed my hair with the hot comb that had to be heated on the stove. My dad would seldom say, "it smells like hamburgers in here," but that's okay because my hair was fried dyed and laid to the side. Okay, maybe not dyed! It just rhymed well. Even though it was total agony sitting in that chair, getting my hair pressed suffering when mom would mistakenly burn my ear, at the end of the day, I did look cute. So, I really didn't mind it at all. As a matter of fact, I looked forward to getting my hair done every week. This was the beginning of, I AM MY HAIR!

85

The moment I had been waiting for was finally here. I was about twelve years old when my dad said, "Okay, Bee…that was my nickname. Are you ready for the big chair?" My face lit up with excitement. "Yes dad, I'm ready!" He'd flap that cape making a loud snap sound and proudly wrap it around me. When most kids are terrified of their first haircut, I was super excited! The buzz sound of the clippers going around my head as my dad would swivel the chair around and around. Finally, the finished product. As he's handing me the mirror, I'm grinning from ear to ear waiting to see the masterpiece. The look on my face was priceless because I had the baddest afro for a twelve-year-old that I had ever seen. It was perfectly round. While my other friends were still sporting pigtails and bows, I was rough and tough with my afro puff.

As I got older, I continued to love my hair. Every strand had to be in place. There was no walking outside and going to the grocery store with bonnets on. I had to represent when I'd leave the house even if it was just running to the store or to get gas. I was the one that had an appointment at the beauty salon every other week for a wash, cut and an occasional touch up or relaxer. Sitting there for hours upon hours. I mainly wore my hair short. I think it's commonly referred to as the Halley Berry cut. I enjoyed experimenting with light colors like blonde and platinum. I remember one time I decided to color my own hair and I figured I would just go to the nearest beauty supply store, pick out the color I want, mix it up, slap it in, and go. After all I can read!! However, this process did not turn out the way I thought it would. Who knew that to mix the right color for your hair you must take into consideration the under tone of your skin? I didn't know; I didn't go to beauty school…I know what you're thinking, *I should have left this to the professionals*. Well, I didn't because that's what we do as women. We like change and we feel we don't have to run to the salon every time we want to change.

I started putting the color in my hair and I could see it working. Slowly, I could see my hair changing and from what I could see, it was looking hot!! I knew I had this! I kept going and it kept lightening. Now for the big reveal! The moment we've all been waiting for. I unveiled the towel from around my head and before I could actually see my hair, I saw the brightest reflection of light. I thought it was my time and I was going home to meet my Heavenly Father. But no, it was actually the reflection beaming from my hair. That's right, my hair looked light a 90-watt light bulb!! This was the last time I did my own hair. At this point, there was nothing I could do because you should not put color on top of color in the same day. Therefore, I had to go to work looking like a bright light!! I was so embarrassed. When the time was right, I quickly made an appointment with my girl at the salon so that she could tone this head down.

After a few years of experimenting with my short cut, I was challenged to grow my hair out. Oh, and how I love a challenge. I bet the girls in the office that I could grow my hair out for two years, untouched other than a wash and occasional clipping of my ends. Here the journey begins. Since my hair was already short prior to the challenge, I had to go through the "ugly" stage of hair growth. Ya'll know this stage. This is the stage where nothing is cute. The hair is even all over, there's no style, there's no "umph" and I am ready to cut it because I have always been about my hair. Once all of the relaxer grew out, I was beginning to feel a little better about growing it out. It grew and grew and grew like wildflowers.

Because my hair was so important to me, I spent a lot of time and money in products for it. I had every product named to woman. I had to figure out what product worked well on my hair type. It was curly and nappy all at the same time. Which reminds me, when I was born my mother told me I had three grades of hair. On top it was curly, on the side it was straight, and, in the back, it was nappy to the huck!! How God saw fit to give me three grades of hair is beyond me. So, back to my hair… I probably spent a few days a week and weekends twisting and making sure every strand was straight. I tried twist outs, the wet n' curly look, the Angela Davis afro look, corn rows, you name it I probably tried it.

After two years had gone by, the challenge was officially over. I, Stephanie the queen of hair, did not cut her hair for two whole years. I couldn't believe it myself. Then one day, I decided to see how long my hair had actually gotten. I went to the beauty salon and the stylist commenced to blow drying and flat ironing it. Oh my GOSH, my hair was to my shoulders. I was slinging that stuff left and right. I think I may have even gotten whip lash!! It was so long, and it was something I had never had. I decided to leave it flat and straight for 30 days.

Again, not knowing what I was doing, you can't just straighten your hair every day and decide, "oh I think I will go back to kinky curly." That was not happening. It was a nightmare! I was back to my baby days, but just more of it. Straight in some places, curly in some and nappy at the roots. It was awful!!! You can probably imagine what I did next. You got it!!! I cut it! I cut it all off. But while the hair was growing, apparently the edges were doing their own thing. Apparently, they didn't want to hang around. So now I have a receding hair line that was not cute. I had no idea what was happening under the veil.

In the process of growing hair, I had gone to the doctor a few years earlier because I had felt a lump in my throat. It turned out that I had a goiter on my thyroid gland the size of a bubble gum golf ball. It didn't hurt, it just felt weird when I swallowed. The doctor said that half of the thyroid had to be removed and that I would have to live on Synthroid for the rest of my life. Synthroid is the medication that will balance the other half of my thyroid so that my metabolism and other organs can work properly. Of course, this was what I needed and wanted. I lived on Synthroid for years and while doing so the synthetic medication was wreaking havoc on my hairline. At that point my hairline was too aggressive to try and grow back and blend. This was when I decided I didn't need it and it was just hair. I'd rather have no hair than to have a receding hair line. That's just me. No shade thrown to women with receding hairlines. This was a choice I made for me, and it was the best choice that I've ever made. When I first cut my hair, I got so much attention. Some was good and some was bad, some thought I was sick and some just thought…WOW! Either way, no matter what they thought, I didn't care. This was who I was. This is who I am. BALD, BOLD, and BEAUTIFUL!!!

Even though the decision to rock my baldness with boldness was easy, I still had some reservations about it. Later, it became a reservation on a spiritual level. I remember being at my job one day and a young lady was telling me that her preacher preached an amazing sermon on Sunday. I said, "Really? Tell me about it." She began to first tell me that her pastor no longer will allow women in the church with their heads uncovered. I began to think, "So I can't attend your church because I'm bald and that I needed to cover my head?" In my head I'm thinking, "I will not be attending your church." The scripture reference was, 1 Corinthians 11:6, ESV: *"For if a wife will not cover her head, then she should cut her hair short. But since it is disgraceful for a wife to cut off her hair or shave her head, let her cover her head"* and that a woman's hair is *her glory.*

Now my spirit is damaged. Being a devout Christian, I love the Lord and praise God in every way, but my head is a disgrace? No way!!! No way will I believe this. There are many scriptures in the Bible as it relates to hair. Whether it's the man's beard, braiding of the woman's hair, whether a woman should cut the natural veil or whether a man should not wear his hair long, I believe today that God gives us free will regarding what we do with our hair and our clothes as long as we're respectful. Hair is a unique part of our bodies that doesn't directly serve a major purpose. We don't need hair to live healthy sustainable lives. The fact that some of us no longer can grow hair in some places or all over, indicates that it must be ok to be bald otherwise God would not have allowed Synthroid to disrupt my hair follicles or other scalp diseases that so many of my BBB friends suffer.

Ladies, God loves us with hair or without hair. He loves every inch of our bodies. Wear your baldness with boldness and be the beautiful woman God created you to be. Stand strong with your heads held high proclaiming your God given beauty!

STEPHANIE WHITE

Stephanie White is a native of Hampton, Virginia. Five years ago, Stephanie met the love of her life on a dating site. Joseph "Joe" White, Jr. has swept her up and moved her to Maryland where she lives with him and their two four legged babies. Stephanie is also the proud mother of a beautiful young lady, Jordan, and an amazing bonus son "Trey." Stephanie and Joe also share the love of his five beautiful children, Darrell, J'Mar, Kristin, Devin, and Jonai.

Stephanie is a graduate of Virginia State University and holds a Bachelor of Arts degree in Commercial Art and Design. She is also a member of Alpha Kappa Alpha Sorority, Incorporated.

Stephanie White is the owner of ENERG-U Fit, where she offers one-on-one personal training, health coaching, and group fitness on-line. Stephanie has been in the health and fitness industry for over 30 years. It started with her own journey to health and fitness. While today she still has challenges in her body, she continues to help others reach their fitness and health goals. Stephanie received her certification from the International Sports Sciences Association as a fitness trainer of all levels. She also has a certification in nutritional health coach from the Institute for Integrative Nutrition. With her knowledge of nutrition and training, she is dedicated to supporting others on their health journey. Stephanie's dream and goal is to change the world one body at a time.

To connect with Stephanie, visit energu.liveeditaurora.com, Bit.Ly/Foodiesnfitness, or email her at energufit@gmail.com.

NO HAIR...DON'T CARE

ᙓ•ᙔ

Juanita Contee

You have Central Centrifugal Cicatricial Alopecia and Traction Alopecia. These were the words told to me by my dermatologist and I thought I was dreaming. In addition, my dermatologist informed me that both types of alopecia were irreversible, meaning any hair that had come out was not going to grow back. She shared with me that I could try different things to help it grow back, but there would be no guarantee that it would grow back and in most cases like mine, the hair doesn't grow back. I literally needed someone to pinch me and wake me from this nightmare. No one and nothing could have ever prepared me for this news. Alopecia? Two types? Me? As if I needed another blow to my emotions, my confidence, and most of all my faith. My thoughts were all over the place and I was afraid.

There weren't too many things that had happened in my life that I couldn't tunnel through, but this seemed insurmountable and unfair. As a woman of faith, I went to God about everything. I trusted Him in all things, and He would reveal to me most times why He was allowing certain things to take place in my life. Allowing alopecia, however, just didn't make any sense and I couldn't understand the significance of it.

95

Hair loss was a phrase I never anticipated would ever be in my vocabulary. I was the girl with incredibly long, thick, kinky tresses. Going to the hair salon as a kid meant being there for what seemed like countless hours for my routine shampoo, press, and Shirley Temple curls because my hair was so thick. But the finished product was always masterful. Mrs. Ella Nichols would press my hair so straight it would look like I had a perm. My Shirley Temple curls were so tight I wouldn't need to wrap my hair at night and my curls were guaranteed to still be in place the next morning.

I can recall growing up hearing conversations about beauty, and in addition to make-up and clothing, hair was always a staple conversation piece when discussing beauty. So, when I started noticing changes with my hair, I felt like my beauty was changing and fading with my hair. I noticed the change while in my first year in college. It started around my edges. They began to thin out as I wore what I thought were protective styles. Braids and cornrows were suitable for me as a first-year college student with a loaded class schedule. With braids and cornrows I could get up and go, then wrap my hair in a scarf or throw on a bonnet at night. It was super convenient and easy for a college student on the go. But each time I removed my braids I noticed my edges would be thinner and thinner. It wasn't a big deal initially, but after it continued to happen with no growth in between styles it became more and more noticeable and apparent that something was wrong. I thought that I was the only one that noticed but others did too, and they were not nice about it.

A young lady that was an associate noticed my thinning edges. She had been laughing about my hair loss around my edges and talking to individuals that were friends of mine unbeknownst to her. My friends reluctantly relayed the news to me that this young lady was laughing about my hair loss, and I was devastated. I cried for several days and was determined to hide my thinning hair at all costs. I wasn't concerned about how much it would cost me or what I had to do. I was going to hide the issue instead of dealing with it because that seemed to be the easiest option. I was determined to never be laughed at again for an issue that I had no control over. I was determined to take control and that's when the years of wearing wigs and weaves began. I had to hide the thinning around my edges and wigs and weaves were my only option.

Several years passed and while wearing wigs and weaves was covering up my hair loss, I had become exhausted with wearing them. I felt trapped and was convinced that there had to be other options for me. I had been going to my hairdresser all these years for wigs and weaves and saw no improvement with my hair. In fact, more hair started to come out. One day my hair stylist noticed a dime size bald spot in the crown of my head. At this point my stylist had done all she could do to try and restore my hair but to no avail. I was frustrated. I thought that if I left my hair alone that perhaps it would grow back, since it had been years since I touched it. This wasn't the case. The hair loss around my edges continued and never grew back and the crown of my head began to thin. My confidence was lower than it had ever been, and I needed to do something else. Hiding and hoping was only frustrating me and my hair continued to fall out.

I remember the day vividly, the day that I grew tired of hiding the condition of my hair. It was draining and frustrating and I felt like my life, time, and energy revolved around hiding. Wigs and weaves are what I used to cover my head during the day while I was out and about, and at night I wore scarves and bonnets. I had become so relentless with hiding the condition of my hair that I would wake up in the middle of the night to make sure my bonnet or scarf had not slipped off. I was afraid that my children would wake up and come into my room at night, as they often did, and see the condition of my hair if my scarf or bonnet slipped off while sleeping. I just could not let that happen. I felt like a prisoner in my own home. I wasn't able to walk around my own home or around my family comfortably because I always had something on my head, and I wouldn't dare leave my head uncovered.

There had to be other options. I couldn't deal with hiding anymore. It was taking over my life. Nothing had become more important than making sure my wig, weave, scarf, or bonnet were near me at all times. One day as I was watching television, I saw an ad about Bosley Hair Restoration, and I called the number and set up a consultation. I was excited that there was a possibility that they could help me, but my excitement was short lived when they showed me the price tag and explained that some pain and discomfort was to be expected. In addition, the crown of my head was an area they wouldn't be able to restore. That was the final straw for me, and I finally found the courage to see my dermatologist to find out what was happening. I felt like a failure, however. I allowed fear and embarrassment to grip me for years and instead of going to see what was happening with my hair early on, I waited and lost valuable time, time that could have been used to save my hair, but instead the hair loss worsened as I hid it.

I was finally ready to face the truth and the diagnosis of alopecia was my truth. Central Centrifugal Cicatricial Alopecia or CCCA is a common cause of alopecia in African American women. Hair loss from CCCA occurs primarily in the central part of the scalp and radiates outward in a circular pattern. The progression of this type of hair loss is usually gradual and causes destruction of the hair follicles resulting in permanent hair loss. Traction alopecia occurs when the hair is being pulled repeatedly or when tension occurs regularly. This type of tension destroys the hair follicles and scarring occurs which prevents hair from growing. Devastated was an understatement. How did I go from a head full of hair to a bald spot in the middle of my head and no edges? It didn't make any sense. I had to find a way to accept my diagnosis and trust the process. Hiding was no longer an option. Hair repair and restoration was no longer an option, and I refused to be depressed, embarrassed, and afraid going forward. Those emotions gripped my life for years and instead of living I was hiding.

I took a moment to pray and ask God for His guidance on this new chapter of my life and how to handle it. I asked Him to show me His will concerning my life and alopecia. It was then that He instructed me to share my diagnosis with my family and close friends and that my desire then was to be bald. I didn't want to be a prisoner any longer to wigs, weaves, and scarves. I wanted to be free and happy and embrace my diagnosis. I knew that if God brought me to this moment, then He had also equipped me to get through it. I called a friend who is a barber and told her what was going on and what I wanted to do. She checked in with me to make sure I was certain about taking it all off, and I couldn't have been any more certain at that moment. I'll never forget July 5, 2020 – the day I cut it all off. My nerves were out of control, but I maintained my focus because I knew for sure that being bald was what I wanted to do. My alopecia was not reversable and my hair was not going to grow back, and I would eventually be bald. When I saw myself for the first time as a baldie, I was pleasantly surprised. I absolutely loved my new look. I had evolved into a more amazing version of myself.

Courage and boldness that I never knew was on the inside of me was revealed.

My only reservation was showing and telling my children. As a mom of five children, two of them being girls, fear gripped me again. How was I supposed to stand before my children as a woman with no hair? They hadn't seen a woman without hair before. I had no clue as to how I would tell them and show them my new look. I began feeling ashamed that my example of womanhood and mommy-hood wasn't going to be typical. I didn't want my children, especially my girls, to be ashamed of me and I didn't want my girls to be fearful that it could happen to them, too. But I pulled on that new confidence and boldness that was revealed and decided to show my children that I was bald.

My girls had many questions and my sons looked at me in shock. I confidently explained as best I could to them what happened to my hair and why I was bald. They all were apprehensive at first, but after some time they began to realize that mommy not having hair was okay. My girls soon came to me and said mom you are still beautiful. My sons have just become used to my look and one of my twin sons, Jude, loves kissing my crown. That's when I knew my confidence had taken over and that I was truly no longer afraid to embrace my truth.

Now, I absolutely love my look. My best friend encouraged me to post a picture of myself on social media as a baldie and the response was explosive. I wasn't expecting the love and positive feedback, but it was the icing on the cake. It was amazing to know that being a baldie was viewed as powerful and a representation of confidence and boldness that goes beyond the norm. I knew then that I could do this, and I am so glad I did. Not only have I evolved and grown but I have helped so many people who had been struggling with alopecia and who now have found their confidence to rock their crowns. I have found strength that I never knew I had, but my confidence to embrace this journey has helped so many others that I never even knew I could reach and that is what means the most to me.

JUANITA CONTEE

Juanita Contee is a singer, songwriter, teacher, preacher, motivational speaker, and mother of five children. She was born and raised in Salisbury, Maryland and currently resides in Baltimore, Maryland. She has been singing since the age of three and preaching since the age of eight. Juanita is the former Minister of Music at the Empowerment Temple AME Church under the former Pastorship of Dr. Jamal Bryant. Juanita made history at Empowerment Temple by being the first female Minister of Music in the history of the church. She was granted the Governor's Citation for her excellent music ability and service at Empowerment Temple and in the AME church.

She currently serves as a leader in the Music Ministry at Celebration Church in Columbia, Maryland. She is an alumnus of

Bowie State University where she studied Fine & Performing Arts, and has completed her Master's Degree in Legal Studies at the University of Baltimore. Juanita is currently obtaining her Doctoral degree in Organizational Leadership from Columbia International University.

Juanita has traveled the world performing and preaching being featured on many stages and award shows such as the Stellar Awards and TBN. Her vocal ability has granted her opportunities to sing with many greats to include Patti Label and Kirk Franklin to name a few. She believes that every journey she's walked was preparation for her next level. To keep in touch with Juanita she can be followed on Instagram and Facebook social media platforms under the name Juanita Contee.

NOW YOU CAN SEE MY FACE

೦ • ೦

SummahLuv Alston

I am SummahLuv Alston! And I Am Alopecia Frontal Fibrosante! I am a Personality-Host/MC, Motivational Speaker, Actress, Community Event Organizer, Chaplain, Advocate, Author and a Full-Figured Model with Alopecia Frontal Fibrosante... just to name a few! I was blessed to be raised in a two-parent home in Brooklyn, New York on February 19, 1962, and I am the third of a gifted and talented blended family of nine children. I taught myself how to sew at the age of 11 and have always had a love for fashion.

At the age of 47, losing my hair (first sited June 25, 2009), I lost a lot of confidence. There is a lot of pressure on women with stereotypes like "a woman's hair is her crown and glory!" So, like many women, I hid behind wigs and weaves. It was in 2018 when I decided to shave my head. It was the best decision that I made. As I studied and researched alopecia (since 2009), I've come to learn that it is a rapidly growing condition that's caused by medications, illness and disease, and stress. The main reason for my alopecia is still undermined. I also realized that men, too, are affected by alopecia and are really having a hard time dealing with male-patterned baldness.

So, let's go back for a moment when I first noticed my alopecia. On June 25, 2009, as the world mourned the loss of Michael Jackson, I was mourning the loss of my hair! For a decade, I adorned a head full of beautiful locs which were colored Honey Blonde and had grown down to my thighs...for the third time! My locs were my pride and joy! Many people refer to locs as dreads. I never allowed anyone to refer to my locs as dreads. No offense to my Rastafarian Brothers and Sisters! The meaning of dread is to; 1) Fear greatly, and 2) Regard with awe. THAT WAS NOT MY HAIR!

Just like many of you, it was devastating to me to see that I suddenly lost the front of my hair. I had no idea what was happening to me all of a sudden. Statistically, we as women are brainwashed to believe that our hair is our *crown and glory*, and our hair is our beauty! So, just like many of you, I always felt beautiful because I always took pride in my hair. It made me feel beautiful, too! I always had a head full of hair. I wore weaves, perms, braided extensions, and then I decided to loc my hair! I cared for and maintained my hair myself. I took pride in my hair; and I wore so many different styles and had so many different looks. My hair was me!

While I was in the middle of loc maintenance, I noticed that each of my locs – along the whole front of my head – were hanging on a string of hair! I had no idea what was happening at the time or what to even call this! I had never even heard of alopecia! I tried to cover the front of my head by shortening the front of my locs with scissors.

Yes, I tried to make bangs...LOL! I looked in the mirror and thought to myself, "Dang, you look like a Japanese Worrier or one of our founding fathers..." LOL! Yes, I laughed to keep from crying! So, when I realized right away that the bang wasn't going to work, I took the scissors and cut all of my hair off! Wow! What am I going to do now?? I am BALD! So, like many of you, I put a scarf on my head, went to the hair store and purchased a wig! The next day when I went to work, I was asked by many of my coworkers, "What happened to your locs?" Of course, I was too embarrassed to tell the truth! So, I replied, "I just needed a change!"

After three years of not understanding or being able to explain why I could not grow my hair back at the front of my hairline, I finally talked to one of my really good friends. She asked me, "Did you see a dermatologist?" I replied, "Duh...a dermatologist?" She said, "Duh, yes! Isn't your hair growing out of your skin? Do you not see a dermatologist for your skin?"

To me all I could do was laugh and say, 'oh yes!!' But that's when I realized and understood that education is very important! So, after being diagnosed finally with alopecia, I began to study and research because I had no clue what it was, what it does, or what caused it. Unfortunately, my alopecia was caused as a result of all of the stress in my life at that time

In January 2019, I was challenged by my best friend to do a model casting call as a full-figured model! I have had the honor and pleasure of meeting Plushy Jenica, walking for several designers, and meeting some amazing people. At the time, I was a *large and in charge shorty* (5 foot 2 inches and around 230 pounds)! So, I went to the casting call, and like many of you, sometimes unsure...even ashamed of my bald head sometimes, I wear hair! I own a lot of wigs! But I opted to do the casting call BALD! To my surprise, I was casted by four designers to walk for their brand! During my moment of surprise and excitement, as I said to each of the designers, "If you would like, I can wear hair! I have a closet full of hair!" Each one of the designers said the same thing, "Oh, no, Queen! You are beautiful just the way you are!" One of the designers even said, "Queen, you are absolutely beautiful! I want you to represent just the way you are! Let the world see your face!"

So, this was the beginning of my second career and most of all...My Passion! I immediately developed and grew a love and passion for modeling and walking in shows. Two years later, Plushy Jenica signed me up as one of her models in January 2021. Plushy Jenica inspired and encouraged me to pursue my passion. Through coaching sessions with Plushy Jenica, I developed confidence on the runway. So, as a model, I represent the Fluffy Queens! At #Over50Almost60... I represent the Seasoned-Citizens! Yes, I Am proud to be a senior! Also, as a result of several traumatic injuries and being a WTC/911 survivor, I, too, represent the *differently-abled*... I Am Disabled! I live in pain every day! Being disabled led to homelessness for 4½ years! But most importantly, I represent the women around the world who look like me... like you...like US…the Alopecia Community! And I knew that this would be a great opportunity to represent as I aspire to inspire!

There are so many women who shave for fashion and beauty; that's not who I am! I don't represent the vain community! There are emotions, tears, hurt, embarrassment we feel after hair loss! This feeling is mutual for men, women, and children alike! The emotional and psychological pain we feel as a result of alopecia is so real. So, I represent for US! Bringing awareness and building confidence through education, the arts, the stage, and fashion is my passion! And that is what I desire to do. So, in October 2018, I established Summah Luv LLC.

In addition to modeling, I own and operate Summah Luv, LLC and Sarah's House of Love, LLC (Hampton, Virginia). I aspire to inspire! There are many forms of and reasons that people are affected by alopecia. Alopecia is a rapidly growing medical condition that has affected so many men and women across the globe. With stigmas that a woman's hair is her beauty, it's been extremely difficult for so many women around the world to deal with. It is a Bold...Bald walk, but someone has to do it! It is my passion to represent the bald, the senior Community, the disabled, and the full-figured!

One day as I was walking through Walmart shopping, I was stopped by a woman. The woman looked in my face and said, "Excuse me, Ma'am...I am not gay, but I think you are absolutely beautiful! Girl, you are rocking that bald head!" As we laughed, she then asked, "Can I please kiss your head?" It doesn't take much for me to entertain an audience! So, I immediately curtseyed and then bowed. And to my surprise, the woman really kissed the top of my head in Walmart! After laughter, we had a long conversation about alopecia and my experience. I am often stopped in the street; I receive inbox messages, and many phone calls from women and men who are going through emotionally due to their journey and experience with alopecia.

I have met the most wonderful and amazing Kings and Queens who are so ashamed of their experience with alopecia. And as I say to them, "This is a bold bald walk! You have to be ready! It's a personal experience!" And I also suggest, when you feel that you are ready, and this is for each and every one of you reading this, it's only when you are ready for this journey, make it special! Celebrate you! Celebrate yourself! Have a celebration and invite family and friends to come over. Let them to know how it has made you feel. Make it a reveal party and show off and rock your crown!

Like so many of you, when I first realized that I was losing my hair in 2009, I felt embarrassed and ashamed, and I didn't want anybody to see me like that. So, I wore wigs and weaves to hide from the reality that I lost the whole front of my hair. I looked in the mirror and really hated what I saw. I looked like a Japanese Worrier or one of our founding fathers. Now don't get me wrong, that look is great for them. However, for me, that didn't work at all. A receding hairline is not the look for me! In December 2018, the rest of my hair began to fall out very badly. I looked in the mirror and said to myself, "Let it go! You had hair when you were young, and it mattered! You're getting older! Either people are going to accept it, or they won't! Let It Go!" I immediately began to shave my head. To my surprise, I received an overwhelming support, love and encouragement from family, friends, and strangers.

On and off social media I often questioned God, "Why Me?" Now, I know why. I believe that God knows His children! God knew that I would be able to take this bold, bald walk and inspire men, women and children who look like me! God knows that I aspire to inspire! And as I have heard from so many men, women, and children alike, I am forever grateful for all of the love and support. So, I will continue to study, learn, educate, and support as I aspire to inspire! And I now know that my hair is not a loss…it's a gain! I have gained confidence as a result of research, studies, understanding, love, and support! I no longer have to feel like I must hide behind wigs and weaves! I have learned how to walk in my baldness because *now you can see my face and my heart*!

SUMMAHLUV ALSTON

SummahLuv Alston retired from the United States Postal Service on disability and is a WTC/911 Survivor. She gave birth to one but is a mother of many. She is a speaker, coach, podcast show host, chaplain, advocate, model, actress, personality host/MC, motivational speaker, mentor, and motivator.

Even though this is her first published work, *My Bald Is Beautiful: I Am Not My Hair*, SummahLuv is working on two more books! She is definitely on the rise! She believes that the world is her school, experience is her teacher and life has taught her some valuable lessons! With all of life's lessons, experiences and journey, trials, and tribulations, SummahLuv will tell you, "The devil don't want me, and God is not ready for me!" She is still here for a reason... Not A Season!

You can follow this aspiring author on social media:

Facebook: I Am SummahLuv

Instagram: @Hair4SummahLuv

TikTok: @IAmSummahLuv1

Twitter: @TogVoy and @LuvSummah

SummahLuv is very passionate, and she hopes to #AspireToInspire

Photography by Ricky Recardo

THE OTHER SIDE

CR • ED

Theresa "Tee" Sudderth

It was 1987 when my sister, June, discovered the first bald spot. "What happened here?" she asked with a puzzled look on her face. She reached out and touched my head with her fingers. 'That's funny,' I thought. I can really feel her touch. I reached to the back of my head and was rendered speechless. OMG! What is that? My skin?? It felt warm and smooth, just no hair. I frantically ran into the bathroom, looked in the mirror... and there it was... A round, smooth, hairless spot about the size of a quarter. It seemingly popped up out of nowhere! There were no hairs in my bed or in the shower. I felt nothing unusual when I combed my hair. What could this be? How long was it there before June noticed it? Had others seen it at work? This totally threw me, and I was stunned.

June tried to comfort me and said it didn't look that bad. She suggested that I comb some of my hair over the spot to cover it up until I get to the doctor. I knew she was saying that to make me feel better, but I also knew covering it would be difficult because I had short hair. The next day I wore a scarf to work (which is not easy to do being that I work in corporate America) and immediately made an appointment with a dermatologist for the following week.

As I was sitting in the waiting room, it seemed to me that everyone could see the spot, which had gotten a little larger by the time my appointment came up. I just wanted to put a magazine over my head. When my name was finally called, I got on my feet and dashed through the door. The nurse showed me to an available room, and I hurriedly sat on the examination table; my anxiety was through the roof. A few minutes went by after the nurse left, then there was a quick knock on the door and in entered a handsome, older gentleman, tall, salt and pepper hair. "Hello! I'm Dr. Stern. Your name looks familiar. Are you related to June Sudderth?" I wanted to say, 'Let's forego the niceties, buddy! I'm a single woman with a HOLE in my head, now FIX IT!!' But my parents raised me right and I held my tongue. "Hello, nice to meet you. Yes, June is my sister." "Ah! I can see the resemblance," he declares brightly. With a tight smile, I reply "Yep, people have said that."

My expression must have indicated to Dr. Stern that his chatty bedside manner was not working. I wanted answers. He asked me why I was there, and I showed him. Dr. Stern proceeded to examine my bald spot. He was very gentle as he looked, poked, and prodded. Nonchalantly, he pulls a stool on rollers from the corner of the room and sits in front of me. He says that I am showing signs of Alopecia Areata, an autoimmune disease which is mistaking my hair follicles as bacteria. This often happens due to stress or a Vitamin D deficiency. However, this was not a severe case. He prescribed a cream for me to use night and day and a follow-up visit in six weeks. Well, it worked. By the time I returned to his office, there were wisps of hair beginning to grow and the hole was slowly closing. In a matter of 3-4 months, there was no sign that the alopecia even existed. The bare patch was gone. I'm normal again and I put this behind me. Thank God for modern medicine.

A few years later, in 1990, I married a charming young man from Senegal, West Africa. June was a beautiful bridesmaid. Three years later, we had our daughter, N'Deye. We were in heaven…or so we thought. A few more years in and the shine started to get a little tarnished and things weren't so heavenly anymore. He wasn't so charming, and neither was I. Our marriage was headed downhill. Nevertheless, for the sake of our daughter, we hung in there.

And lo and behold, the bald spots were back and with a vengeance. This time there were two large patches near the top of my head. Well, I went running back to Dr. Stern. The diagnosis was the same as before, but because they were so big, he felt this situation warranted another more aggressive type of treatment. He treated me with very painful shots of steroids directly into those bald spots for several weeks. I wanted my hair back at any cost. This time, we knew it was stress contributing to this latest bout. And it did not help that I was very anemic because of fibroids and heavy periods. It took longer this time for the patches to fill in, so I decided to get braids on the hair that was not affected and placed them strategically to hide this embarrassment. It went back and forth like this for a number of years…a bald patch one day, get shots, it grows back, rinse and repeat.

In 2000, I had the latest set of braids taken out. There were no patches and my hair had grown considerably! Joy! So, I decided to try something new and have my hair twisted to start dread locs. It took six months for my hair to fully lock, but it was worth it. I loved them and within three years, I was literally sitting on my locs; they were perfect for my overall aesthetic and personality.

But in the spring of 2002, my world was ripped out from under my feet and turned upside down. June, my dear sister, was diagnosed with cancer. Four months later, at the age of 48, she passed away. My family and I were emotionally distraught. Along with my devastation, I became very angry with God. I carried that anger with me a long time. In 2006, my dad passed away. Then in 2011, my brothers, Billy, Philip, and I said goodbye to our mom. Over a period of nine years, our close-knit family was shattered.

Thanksgiving of the next year rolls around and one of my BFFs, Helen and I went on a much-needed cruise. As we were getting ready for a fun night out, she noticed that the hair line in the back of my head was very high. When I placed my hand back there, it wasn't just a patch this time. The whole lower half of my hair was gone. The hairline in the back was no longer at the nape of my neck it had moved to the middle of my head. I couldn't BELIEVE it. Well, thank God my locs were thick and long so they were able to cover the blank space. This was not going to deter me from having a good time. There was a lot of fun to be had, things to do and the bartender at the salsa lounge knew to keep my glass filled with Bailey's Irish Cream Whiskey.

When I returned home, I thought about what I was going to do about my hair. I knew the course my doctor would take, and I didn't want those shots. The larger the area the more of those painful injections I would have to endure and who wants that? So, I made a conscious decision to relax, and treat this alopecia with any concoction I could find or buy on the internet in the hopes that my hair would grow back. Well, that did not work at all. And slowly, but surely, not only did my beautiful locs begin to fall out one-by-one, the rest of the hair on my whole body was disappearing; eyebrows, eyelashes, underarms, and every other place one can imagine where there is hair. By the summer of 2014, there were approximately seven or eight locks remaining.

One day, Dale, my good friend and co-worker with whom I ate lunch with every day, asked me, "Tee, how many locs do you have now?" "Three," I replied quietly. "I just wrap them around my head and put on a stocking cap to keep them in place before putting on a wig or a scarf." He asked, "why I don't just take them out?" Looking down, I told him "Because it's all I have left. I don't want to let them go." A week or two went by and he asked again, "Tee, how many

119

locs do you have now?" With a tear in my eye, I responded softly, "One." I wiped my eyes with a napkin, sniffling and continued to look down, embarrassed. Gently he whispered, "Tee, it's done. Just take it out." Deep down, I knew he was right. So, that evening, with a heavy sigh, resolute and solemn, I slowly pulled out the last loc. Everywhere that hair could grow, was gone now. From head to toe, I was hairless, and I am absolutely God-smacked.

To make matters worse, the next day my supervisor called me into an office where she stated that due to reorganization within the company, I was being laid off. Nine years of dedicated service…gone.

Coming to terms with my new unwanted external look was challenging to say the least. Further research indicated that I had the most advanced form of alopecia called Alopecia Universalis, the complete loss of hair on the scalp and body. At this time, my husband and I were separated, my daughter was in college 3½ hours away in Baltimore, Maryland, and my mother and sister were not around to administer advice, nurture me, or give support. I was on my own. Scarves and wigs were part of my everyday attire and I hated it. The only time I would look into a mirror was if my head was completely covered.

Six weeks later, on my last day of work, I took a week-long vacation, alone. A good friend gave me her timeshare at a resort up in The Berkshires of Massachusetts, a very rural quiet area. Here is where I contemplated and meditated on what to do next; where was I headed. I am bald… completely hairless and I can't think of how to move forward. What did I WANT to do? The only thing I did know was that I did not want to go back to corporate life. So, I started from there and began to research information regarding virtual assistant work. Encouraged by what I found, I created a virtual admin assistant business, gave it a name, and began working from home. Not a bad idea and I gained several clients. But I realized that I'm not the go-getter that a business truly needs to be successful. Nevertheless, I worked hard and gained new acquaintances along the way. One of my clients became a close friend and in 2015, he was instrumental in encouraging me to actually see my beauty…I mean REALLY see it, to look at my inner qualities; for there's more to beauty than hair.

Feeling a little better about myself (and I really did not want to go through another New York summer with my head covered up!) on Sunday, June 28, 2015, I invited my close friends and family to my home where I took off my scarf and revealed my bald head. They were so supportive and happy for me. It was an amazing feeling. The next day, I posted pictures on Facebook announcing to everyone else about my new look. Well, the comments were astounding. I never knew people felt the way they did about me. It was truly uplifting. This became my new "birth" date!

However, shortly thereafter and despite my alopecia, a number of other issues arose – mortgage problems and major financial issues. I knew something had to be done but, again, I didn't have any answers. So, while standing in my kitchen, I had a serious, outpouring, ugly crying, gut wrenching, garment twisting, soul searching, *come-to-Jesus meeting* with God. There was a lot said, but at the end of the day, I simply asked Him for help. The very next day, miracles began to happen in my favor, and over the next several months, they kept happening, over and over. Let's just say my "problems" were answered, some completely and some were made bearable. Won't He do it!!

In addition, in 2019 at the age of 59, I decided to pursue my lifelong ambition as an actress. I had pictures taken, developed my resume and set up a profile on Backstage.com. Two weeks later, I was asked to audition for an off-off-Broadway play, and I landed the part. They saw past my hairless aesthetic and saw my talent, confidence, and a beauty that I didn't know I had. I went on to do two more plays, a number of background roles in several television shows, two independent movie projects, and two commercials for the same company. I was living my real dream and was very happy.

Which brings me to the title of this chapter. Every experience I encountered during my hair loss had a purpose. With all the difficulties of coming to terms with this disease, I persevered. I discovered on the other side of this adversity that my confidence was not about my hair. My femininity was not about my hair. My talent as an actress was not about my hair. My sexiness was SO not about my hair. Being a mother, a daughter, a sister, a friend, a co-worker was not about my hair. So, today, I have thoroughly embraced my hairless head and body. Unbeknownst to me at that time, that very first bald spot in 1987 was the start of my journey so I could truly know what freedom feels like and hopefully be an encouragement for others.

With God's grace, He got me through to the other side.

THERESA "TEE" SUDDERTH

Theresa "Tee" Sudderth is a lifelong resident of Westchester County, New York; 30-minutes north of Manhattan. She is the youngest of four siblings, an actress, a former wife, a cancer survivor, a corporate assistant, and a mother.

As the child of artistic parents (her father was a musician in the Big Band era and her mother was a painter and a vibrant elocutionist of poetry), Theresa, aka Tee, was magnetically drawn to the performing arts. Tee became an active member of the following workshops/theatre groups: The Loft Film & Theatre School; The Renaissance Drama Co.; WISE Drama Workshop, and WCC Drama.

She worked as a secretary during the day and performed in plays or attended workshop classes at night. However, with life's consistent challenges, working in the office became her trade and sole source of income. For 40 years, Tee became a leading executive administrative assistant in many Fortune 500 companies. As an entrepreneur, Tee developed/owned a virtual assistant service and an event planning business. She followed her parents into Masonic Life and joined the Order of Eastern Star, achieving the highest position in the chapter as Worthy Matron.

Tee is also a former member of these organizations: PTA Council, Girl Scout Association, Greenburgh Education Committee, and the Fairgrounds Civic Association. Currently she is an active member of the Golden Apple Chorus, an a cappella singing group. Her hobbies are reading, cooking, crocheting and indoor gardening. Tee is divorced, has re-ignited her acting career and is a proud mother of N'Deye, her daughter.

Profile Link: https://www.backstage.com/u/tee-sudderth/

Email: miztee717@gmail.com

My Bald Is Beautiful: I Am Not My Hair

126

TRANSFORMED BY ALOPECIA

CƷ•ℰ

Shurvone Wright

Have you ever gone through a period in your life when a life-changing experience presented itself and you were changed forever? In those moments you have a choice to embrace the change and grow from it or stay stuck in the fear of the change. For most of my childhood and young adult life, I had so many life-changing experiences that created lots of fear and insecurities that carried into my adulthood. So, for many years I fought against those little voices in my head that told me I was never good enough, I was not pretty enough, or smart enough. The crazy part was I would always manage to do things I wanted, but never really resting in the power of who I knew I could be. I was never really settled in many of my decisions in life. I was always waiting for something bad to happen, not certain things would turn out the way I wanted. So, I did not live to my fullest potential; I was uncertain, scared, and insecure.

All our life experiences are woven through a journey to make us into who we are. I truly believe my journey in life has transformed me into the person I am today. I have become a woman that has chosen to embrace and stand boldly being bald. I wanted to share with you how my life experience has helped me embrace being bald and unafraid to show up in the world to express myself in a way that brings life to my soul.

I truly believe that something happened before I was nine years old that formed the shy personality that developed throughout my life. You might ask why I chose nine years old. It seems that I can't remember anything before I was nine, except when I was five years old, I was left alone in a home where I lived, and I don't remember why I was standing alone standing near the front door crying. I remember feeling scared and alone. The experience is so vivid, that when I think about it 56 years later, I can feel the fear in my gut. I can visually see what seemed like a very large and scary place, feeling overwhelmed. As a child, of course, I just felt scared, but as an adult, I can attach the words overwhelmed and alone.

When I was nine years old, my grandfather died. He was my father figure and when he died, I remember thinking my life would be very different and I felt a deep sense of uncertainty and not feeling protected from the world. These were two very significant times in my life that have been embedded in my subconscious, that has played a part in my insecurities and fears. I have never connected the two experiences or realized how they have affected my life and formed who I had become, but I can see how those experiences have changed my life.

I went through life very shy and always felt invisible around family and friends. I know you might be thinking, *where is she going*

128

with this story? I thought she was going to tell me about being bald and beautiful. I want to do my best to paint a picture for you so you can understand how God has truly formed my life and how He can transform your life. He can turn what the enemy tries to use against you to destroy you, but God uses it to transform you.

As I grew into a young woman, I always had a deep knowing that I was better than any negative situation that presented itself. I always knew I wanted to have a life I would be proud of, and I would be something special, leaving a mark on the world. Over many years I struggled with wanting people to like me. I wanted to fit, however, I never fit in. I did not have many friends in school. I never participated in any type of group activities. I honestly don't know how I made it through high school, other than it was God watching over me. I grew up allowing men to treat me any way they wanted, and I accepted every unacceptable behavior and treatment because I did not know my worth and value. As I mentioned before, I always found a way to rise above horrible situations that normally would take another person down. I now know it was God giving me the strength, the wisdom, and knowledge to come out of a bad situation.

My life however took a bad turn when I turned 18 years old. I allowed my insecurities and the need to be liked to overrule my better judgment. My boyfriend at the time was on drugs, and one night I allowed him to talk me into trying drugs and my life took a very bad. I went on a downward spiral for two years straight using drugs and living a life that should have killed me; however, I knew in my soul there was more for me to do.

One morning after being up all-night doing drugs, I heard in my spirit "you're going to die if you don't stop." I called a woman at my job who would always tell me if I needed her to call her. I don't ever remember her giving me her number or how I reached out, but I did call her for help. She picked me up, took me to her church; we all prayed, and I accepted the Lord in my life. I remember going to church, and not knowing what I would do next. I just went to church for a while where I felt safe. I did not have anywhere to live other than to live with the boyfriend that introduced me to drugs. Again, God was watching over me because I had befriended a woman that introduced me to a program that would introduce me to an amazing nursing program, that would produce a 31-year nursing career and I am still happily serving in the medical profession.

After I finished nursing school, I got married to a man who turned out to be very verbally abusive and later physically. After being married two years, I got the courage to leave. He went to work one day, and I just took what clothes and important papers I could fit in a few boxed and I left. It took a few years to finalize the divorce, but thank goodness we did not have children together, so it was easy.

Three years later, I married my amazing husband, and we started a family. We have been married for 28 years with three beautiful daughters. When you are raising girls they become your focus, and everything becomes about them. We did not have much, so whatever resources we had went to the girls. So, when they were very young, I started wearing wigs and getting my hair braided to make my life easier. As the girls got older, and they needed or wanted to have certain things, I decided I had to give up a few pleasures. So, I started wearing wigs *almost always*, then later it became *always* to the point people did not know what my natural hair looked like.

During their early years, I did not spend much on wigs, but as our financial situation changed, I would spend hundreds of dollars. I wore them so often; I was embarrassed not to wear them because the new people in my life did not know me without them and everyone else got used to seeing me in them. I felt pretty most of the time, but there were times I did not because I was concerned about the quality of the hair, and how it made me look. Wearing wigs was easy, but hard at the same time.

Fast forward to 2020 when the COVID-19 hit the world and we were all in the pandemic together. I thought okay, *I will give my hair a break; I am working from home and will only wear wigs if I must go out.* 2020 was a very stressful and challenging time. I worried about so many things and being on lockdown was so overwhelming; going to the grocery store was overwhelming.

February 2021 my daughter braided my hair a few months prior, so I could wear a wig. One night, I had this vivid dream about a beautiful butterfly on my back and I remember being at peace about it. I am still trying to figure out what it really meant. Three days later, I took my braids out and I noticed my hair was thin; I had never seen it so thin. However, my hair had been thinning over the last year, but this was different. So, I just decided at that moment to shave my head bald. It was strange once I shaved it. In that moment I felt free, I felt beautiful. I decided very quickly that I liked what I saw, so a few days later I shared a picture on my social media platforms, and BOOM!! My friends and family embraced me and loved me for being brave. I was shocked at the love and encouragement I received from so many people, even strangers. I was in awe of the display of love. It took me several months to come to terms with why people seemed so impressed with my bravery. I realized that it was not just bravery that just happened, but bravery that was groomed inside of me over time and because of my life's journey.

I have been transformed into a person that has accepted her inner beauty, and I love who I have become...A woman that has truly fallen in love with her authentic self. I have embraced my baldness. I am not afraid to go out in public, to go to church, to speak on webinars, or Zoom. I am having fun shopping and learning how to update my wardrobe to go along with my new look.

I finally went to the doctors to have an official diagnosis on record of Tractions Alopecia. I was not surprised nor bothered by the diagnosis. It just made it official. I have had a transformation of my inner beauty that transfers to my outer beauty. I feel free to be me. Being bald is such a vulnerable place to be, but at the same time it is a very confident place to be. I feel more beautiful than I have in my life. I am not ashamed of being diagnosed with alopecia. I am not interested in trying to grow my hair back. I am not sure how it would grow back or if that was possible. I am okay with who am and how I look.

I want to ENCOURAGE anyone reading my JOURNEY to be encouraged and know that your hair does not define you. If you are bald by choice, or by a diagnosis know that you are beautiful. Your journey is not just for you; it is also meant to encourage someone else. So, show up in the world and share your journey, share your courage. When you are brave and embrace who you are, it helps others to do the same. I also want to encourage anyone going through the alopecia journey to continue to bring awareness to the world. We need to let our lights shine bright.

Remember to view all your life's experiences as a transformational journey. God would not have you go through anything and then not use the experience for your good. This might be easier said than done; however, if I can do it and come out on the other side and land on my feet feeling beautiful, so can you. So, STAND UP, STAND TALL, AND STAND BOLDLY IN YOUR BALDNESS. You are all BEAUTIFUL.

SHURVONE WRIGHT

Shurvone Wright is an author, speaker, mentor, and founder of Confidence Without Regret – The Butterfly Experience and CEO of La' BossPreneur Marketing, LLC. She encourages women to stand in their truth, helping them to find their voice, to go after their dreams and goals unapologetically. She has a gift of encouragement and exhortation, changing lives across the country.

She is a best-selling author of five books *Courageous Women Find Strength During the Storm* and *Women Who Soar, Finding Joy in the Journey,* and *The Unstoppable Warrior Women* and *For Such A Time This.* She has had the honor of speaking on several radio shows, appearing in multiple magazine ads to promote and discuss her journey and books. She is currently the social media contributing content writer of OWN IT digital magazine.

Shurvone helps entrepreneurs who have a passion to grow their business using social media and business strategies to attract their ideal clients. She helps you to be unafraid to be your best self to elevate your business and your life through her business and her Facebook group called "La Bosspreneur Marketing Society" and her Coaching Program.

Shurvone is the CEO of Everything Wright, LLC. She currently has in production, the company's first product "Bed Budeezy," a unique item she created that will be convenient, affordable, multipurposeful, and supports COVID-19 safety protocols.

Contact Shurvone at shurvonepwright@gmail.com

Shurvone Wright
Author | Speaker | Coach | Thought Leader
CEO La' BossPreneur Marketing, LLC
CEO Everything Wright, LLC

My Bald Is Beautiful: I Am Not My Hair

About the Visionary

Cℨ•℈Ↄ

Michele Irby Johnson

Michele Irby Johnson is a retired, disabled Veteran who is an Energetic Motivational and Transformational Speaker and Trainer as well as a Certified Life Coach who is a much sought-after voice who serves the Abused, Women, Non-Profits, Family and Education, Veterans, and Faith-Based communities through her unique style that reaches deep into the hearts and lives of those longing for transformation, elevation, inspiration, and empowerment. Michele has a great love for seeing people's lives changed. Through speaking, training, coaching, and mentoring, she gets joy in developing and elevating people to a place of greatness, seeing them reach their goals, and helping them to see their tomorrow through the lens of who they were called to be in this world.

As a speaker and trainer, Michele commands the stage to captivate her audience through animated storytelling, humor, wisdom, and authenticity. She understands that she is on the platform to impart and to transfer what the audience needs beyond the conclusion of the event. She injects herself into the moment and shifts the atmosphere prompting listeners to decide what is important to them, how they should respond, and if they want to enact change in their lives or in the businesses.

Michele is the visionary for the **Arise and Inspire Speaker's Bootcamp** which provides a four-day/eight-hour intensive experience where amateur speakers can learn the tools and techniques needed to mount the stage as a speaker. Once attendees have completed the bootcamp, they are invited to participate in the two-day **Arise and Inspire Speaker's Summit**, where they share their stories before an in-person and virtual audience, with opportunities to acquire speaking engagements, new clients, and a connection to a network of experienced speakers.

Michele's gift as a transformation architect has afforded her the opportunity to serve surrounding regions through speaking, preaching, retreats, conferences, and teaching workshops and seminars on Domestic Violence to such groups as educators, medical personnel, clergy, women's ministries, and youth alike. Her capacity has allowed her travel and serve in such areas as Maryland, Washington, DC, Virginia, North Carolina, Alabama, Tennessee, Florida, Texas, Guam, Southwest Asia, and Africa.

As a survivor of Domestic Violence and an advocate against Domestic Violence, Michele penned her first literary work entitled *"Love's TKO: A Testimony of Abuse, Victory and Healing,"* which shares her experiences as a victim of a love gone bad through domestic violence. To continue her love for writing and reaching others through this gift, she has penned her second literary work entitled *"Grace For Your Journey: Sermons of Survival in the Wilderness."* She is a best-selling Co-Author of the anthology *"Women Inspiring Nations Volume 3: I'm Still Standing."* She was the visionary on the anthology projects *"In Recovery: Rising From the Ruins"* released in June 2021 and *"Boots and Beyond: Stories of Trials, Tragedy, Triumph, and Transition"* that was released in November 2021. She has several other literary works in progress that she believes will prove beneficial to all readers from personal, emotional, and spiritual perspectives.

As an educator, Michele has served as an Adjunct Professor at a local university, teaching Health & Wellness classes to undergraduate students; and teaching Counseling Women and Domestic Violence Crisis Counseling (two courses she wrote) to graduate students. She is also passionate about helping people be administratively prepared for the inevitability of death. As a bereavement liaison and consultant, she has written and delivers Estate Planning webinars and workshops to specialized groups, organizations, churches, families, and individuals. She firmly believes that having such affairs in order is a great display of a legacy of love one can leave behind for their families. Her vision is to provide peace of mind for your future.

Michele holds five degrees: Master of Arts in Counseling (Crisis Response and Trauma); Master of Arts in Human Resource Development; a Bachelor of Science in the field of Human Resource Management; as well as two Associates Degrees from the Community College of the Air Force: One in Education and Training and the other in Social Services. She retired from the USAF after 26 years of combined dedicated military service with the 113th DC Air National Guard at Andrews Air Force Base. Michele is affiliated with Veterans-N-Transition, Transformation Academy, Apostolic Grace Evangelistic Fellowship, Speaker Hub, Fair Consulting, Association of Christians in Leadership (Advisor), Black Speakers Network, and Elevation Entourage to name a few. She also hosts her own Virtual Talk Show: *"Life Matters with Michele,"* which airs weekly on Facebook LIVE and is also posted on her YouTube Channel Life Matters with Michele TV Official.

In April 2020, Michele started the Grace Point Radio Broadcast with her husband, Apostle Shaun P. Johnson, Sr. on the DMV Power

Gospel Radio Network. She now broadcasts **Grace Point** on its own YouTube Channel Grace Point TV Official and on Sensational Sounds Radio weekly, both platforms taking to heart the necessity to spread the Gospel to all the world in hopes of introducing the lost to Jesus Christ, reclaiming the backslider, and to minister comfort, strength, encouragement, and healing to the brokenhearted.

As an entrepreneur, Michele's countless skills translate beyond her speaking, training, and coaching arenas as she helps entrepreneurs, educators, authors, clergy, institutions of higher learning, and community leaders to realize their vision by providing virtual assistant services that ease the burden of the cumbersome, day-to-day tasks that often hinder forward movement and success. Her goal is to get individuals and organizations back to productivity and profitability by adding value to their lives through time and project management, administrative support, and curriculum and training development.

As a springboard to their love for literary work, Michele and her husband have launched a self-publishing consulting business that helps authors to fulfill their dream of being published. They offer design services, project management, editorial services, and more.

In her spare time, Michele enjoys watching HGTV, the Golden Girls, and any type of Cold Case, Forensic Files, or crime shows and spending time with her husband, Shaun P. Johnson, Sr. Together, they have three sons, one daughter, and one grandson.

ଓ • ଃ

CONNECT WITH MICHELE

Facebook/LinkedIn: Michele Irby Johnson

Instagram: Michele.irby.75

www.iam-mij.com

www.optimumpvs.com

www.onekingdompublishing.com

www.livingbygraceministries.org

www.kingdomcbi.org

YouTube: Grace Point TV Official

YouTube: Life Matters with Michele TV Official

OTHER LITERARY WORKS BY THE VISIONARY

ଓଃ • ଃ୦

Love's TKO:
A Testimony of Abuse, Victory and Healing

Grace for Your Journey:
Sermons of Survival in the Wilderness

ଓଃ • ଃ୦

VISIONARY ANTHOLOGY PROJECTS

In Recovery: Rising From the Ruins
Stories of Restoration and Resilience

Boots and Beyond:
Stories of Trials, Tragedy, Triumph and Transition

ଓଃ • ଃ୦

CONTRIBUTING AUTHOR

Women Inspiring Nations – Volume 3:
I'm Still Standing